D1556887

The Painter's Widow

L.S. JOHNSON

WITHDRAWN

NILES DISTRICT LIBRARY

This is a work of fiction. All characters and events portrayed in this book are either fictitious or used fictitiously.

Copyright ©2020 by L.S. Johnson. All rights reserved.

Traversing Z Press
San Leandro, California
www.traversingz.com

ISBN (paperback): 978-0-9988936-5-5
ISBN (ebook): 978-0-9988936-6-2
Library of Congress Control Number: 2020909947

Quoted excerpts in this book are from *Henry V* and Sonnet 60, by William Shakespeare

TABLE OF CONTENTS

None is so fierce that dare stir him up:
who then is able to stand before me?
—Job 41:10

CHAPTER I

Letters

J t is one of the curious things about living your life on a precipice: that there are days that are simply lovely, with a cloudless blue sky and warm, dry breezes, gentle enough to ruffle the hair of the woman you love as she spreads a blanket for you. An entire day moving at the drowsy pace of your easy partnership as you talk about gardens, or horses, or the funny story you overheard in the village. An entire day of fingers twining, of lips touching.

An entire, lovely day, at once whole and slow and yet eggshell-fragile, as all days are. Because you know how swiftly such peace can shatter; because you cannot help but wonder what horrors lie behind the most innocent of exchanges, what monstrosities lie behind your neighbors' doors or in their basements.

Since we returned from Medby I did everything I could to forget. I told Mr. Smith no more; I told Jo no more, and she did not argue as she might have done. I busied myself with paying the last of my father's debts and caring for him and Jo alike. I told myself I would be fine, as Mr. Morrow had assured me—

—but to think of him was to remember again, and when

I remembered I dreamed: of the vast creature called Leviathan, of the man I had murdered, of the terror on the boat and my body sailing through the air like I was nothing and that great eye *seeing* me.

I tried to forget, and I avoided the merest glimpses of our bay. I looked away when Mrs. Simmons ladled out anything reddish-brown, lest I remember the blood that had run over my skin; I sent Mr. Simmons or Jo to the butcher, lest I remember how the knife felt when it gouged the man's throat—

Not *man,* but Cutler. That was what Mr. Morrow had called him.

I went to church every Sunday, and when I saw an altercation in the village, or read about an outrage of violence in the papers, I held my hand rigid so as not to form an instinctive fist.

Several months ago I had practiced that fist, practiced it and more besides, telling myself I was an adventuress, a pirate like the ones I had thrilled to learn of in my childhood. Only now did I understand the dark price of such adventures. That there were monsters in the world frightened me; that I had so easily matched their violence terrified me.

And yet there were days like this one, when everything felt almost right: when my father had enough energy to join us at breakfast and hold a conversation, when Jo insisted we leave the house and take some time to enjoy the day, leading me over the soft hills I knew so well. When the blue sky and sweet-smelling grasses lulled me into a brief but deep sleep that seemed to breathe life back into my body.

And when I opened my eyes again, Jo was smiling down at me. "There you are," she said. "Now you look more like yourself."

I feared even to speak, that I might shatter this day, and instead pressed close. Her coat smelled of the grass and the wind and herself. It was her favorite now, a longer, fuller coat of grey wool that softened the men's suits she wore, just as her longer hair softened her face. I knew the latter was a favor to me, for though she preferred it shorn I loved its wild thickness. A small gesture, but one that provoked me to a gratitude bordering on maudlin.

"Your father does better when you feel better, Caro," she continued. Her fingers played with mine, curling and un-curling them. "You help him when you help yourself."

"I know," I whispered. For I did know: she was right, as she was right in so many things. Caring for my father meant I had to be at my best. My moods could lighten or dark-en his, could make the difference between eating well and nibbling fitfully, between joining us downstairs and staying moodily in his bed.

And I needed him to be well. Not just for his sake, though I loved him so dearly it hurt sometimes to think on it, but to give Jo more time to save us. He had returned from Medby so deeply tired I thought I might lose him, and only then had he confessed to me the truth of my circumstances: that our house was entailed to a cousin in New Holland, and the man was eager for it. Once my father passed, I would not only lose my surviving parent and thus my family, but my home as well. Jo was using her father's colleagues to try and alter the entailment, but I suspected it was a hopeless endeavor.

Blood and horror behind me, a life adrift before me. But still, there were these lovely, fragile days.

We returned to the house slowly, pausing to gather a handful of wildflowers which Jo put in a vase to adorn our dinner. Mrs. Simmons was laying out the dishes, mostly lighter fare as heavier foods upset my father's stomach now. Mr. Simmons I saw through the window, talking to a man about the drainage in our lower field. A routine act of management, yet I could not help but feel a small frisson of resentment that such work would only benefit my unknown, greedy cousin.

"You and I," Jo said, "should travel a little. Not far," she amended. "Just to Sunderland. There is a lawyer there who renegotiated an entailment, it would be useful to have him recount his argument. And we could find some new books for your father—perhaps even take in a concert?"

"Perhaps," I said, but I touched my head to hers. "Let me speak to Mister Simmons first."

"Let us both speak to Mister Simmons," Jo said, "so that you do not hear one thing and decide you've heard something else. The last time I proposed an outing," she continued at my frown, "all he did was say the weather looked to turn, but you told me he said your father's lungs were aching from the damp."

"But the damp affects him—"

"Did we even have damp?" she interrupted.

"No," I admitted, then quickly added, "but if it rains it always gives him a cough, and it makes his hip worse—"

"Both of which the Simmonses are able to treat." She drew me to a corner of the dining room, looking deep into my eyes; despite my churning emotions I felt myself weaken as I always did. Would I never stop feeling like a lovesick girl when she looked at me so?

"He does better when you're better," she said in a low, earnest voice. "He takes his cue from your moods. Taking a few days for yourself allows him to have a holiday as well, through you. How much does he love hearing about the village, or when we're able to get news from London? A few days away will give him a month of entertainment."

I told myself it was her implacable reasoning that was making me nod, but when she looked at me like that, oh! I might agree to anything. Before I could respond, though, Mrs. Simmons came in with a small roast, and behind her Mr. Simmons helped my father teeter into the dining room and settle in his chair.

Shall I tell you of my father now? The Theophilus Daniels who had raised me, I had lost in the terrible events surrounding Harkworth Hall, when our dearest friends betrayed us and nearly killed him. The man who took his place had lost his facility of speech, his easy movements; yet there was also a greater kindness in him than I had previously known— and a thirst for adventure, too.

Since Medby, however, my father had changed yet again.

The catarrh he developed in our last days there had never quite left him. He was cold, always, even with the warmth of spring upon us now he wore layers of clothing and demanded blankets wherever he settled. Our dining room was bathed in afternoon sunlight and a low fire burned in the grate; still Mr. Simmons was tucking a blanket over his lap.

That depth of kindness had remained, though now it was occasionally marred by irritation over small matters, like a light turned too bright, or if we read aloud too softly. I was more patient with this than Jo, though their little arguments seemed to rally him as my cajoling never did.

But most concerning of all was the sense of distance he had begun to emanate. Often now his gaze became unfocused, as if seeing a distant horizon invisible to us. The entailment, too, seemed to concern him less as time went on. At Jo's last update he had merely waved his hand and murmured that we would settle it—as if such worldly matters were no longer his concern.

He's leaving me, I had wept from the comfort of Jo's arms that night. *He's leaving me, and he does not seem to care.* And she had comforted me as best she could, but she could offer nothing to counter what I knew was close to hand.

Now, however, the object of so much anguished concern asked for tea, and the butter to be applied to his bread. He wanted a napkin under his chin and the drapes to be opened, then closed some, then opened a little more, all tasks that Mr. Simmons accomplished with enviable patience.

"You two were out so early this morning, you missed the post," Mrs. Simmons said, bustling in with a wad of letters. "And here's the paper if you want to continue on from yesterday."

"Would you like that, sir?" Jo asked. "We could finish the article on the new enclosure scheme."

My father swallowed, licked his lips, then eloquently declared, "pah."

"It's a hard thing for some of the farmers around these parts," Mr. Simmons said.

And there was a time when Theophilus Daniels would have agreed, and lectured us all on the history of grazing rights and its place in shaping the English character. Now he just snorted and ate his toast with vigor. I had no memory of my grandparents, and the elderly in the village were neighbors I greeted and conversed briefly with, but little more. This sense of age, of decline—sometimes it overwhelmed me.

Instead I busied myself with sorting our letters. Our usual bills, a few for Jo from London that I passed to her without scrutiny. Though she had settled with us, she still maintained the fiction of being Jonathan Chase, executor of her father's estate and maintaining an interest in his legal firm. There were always papers for her to review and sign.

At the bottom of the pile was a small, crisp envelope, addressed to

Misses Chase & Daniels

in a hand that I knew far too well. My blood turned to ice, my fingers became nerveless. I was suddenly, furiously angry. *No more*, I had told Mr. Smith after Medby. It seemed, however, that my injunction had been ignored.

I opened my mouth to tell Jo, but she was already reading

her own correspondence—and did she even need to know? After Medby she had left the decision to me, and I had said no. She had not indicated her own position had changed. Therefore I would simply reply in the negative to whatever he proposed, and forget all about whatever terrible prospect he would have us face.

Decided, I shoved the offensive letter deep in my pocket, and set myself to ignoring it.

"Good riding day," my father opined, looking out the window.

I smiled at this regular ploy. "By which I take it you would like a turn in the carriage?" Under the table I nudged Jo with my foot. "I think we can manage that."

But Jo did not respond. She was fixed upon the letter in her hand, and I realized that her face had gone pale. She was nearly as white as her cravat. "Jo?" I asked in a quieter voice.

She blinked and looked at me, and for a terrible moment it was as if she was gazing at a stranger, and then she shook herself. "Ah, no—not for me today. I must respond to this." She nodded, as if agreeing with herself. "If you'll excuse me," she added.

"Jo, are you—"

But she was already gone, the door swinging shut behind her. I found myself staring at her plate with its congealing food. The look in her eyes—! It was a stark contrast to the warmth of earlier. And the tone in her voice—

My father poked my hand with his spoon. When I looked at him he jerked his chin at the door. "Go on," he said.

"She did not seem to want—"

"*Go*," he urged, then went back to eating his soup.

Slowly I rose, working my skirts free from under the table. My father was now wholly focused on his bowl and the Simmonses were elsewhere. I felt alone, and filled with dread. Mr. Smith's envelope a weight in my pocket, and Jo—oh, we had not been together so very long, but in the months of our companionship I would have sworn that she had kept nothing from me. She had received difficult news from home before: debts run up by her mother, a fever suffered by her sister, problems with a man at the firm who her father had favored. Always she had told me about them at once; always she had invited my opinion.

What could she have read that would make her turn away from me?

I went upstairs with a heavy heart and a leaden stomach. The sight of her closed door did nothing to ease my worries. I told myself I was being foolish—it was only my nerves, strained by the entailment and my lingering memories, coloring my judgment now.

When I knocked, however, it was some time before I heard the floorboards creak, and when Jo opened the door her face was drawn. Before I could speak she touched my arm.

"Caro, I'm not feeling well," she said. Her eyes were looking at my face, yet she would not directly meet my gaze. "I think it best if you take your father riding, while I rest this afternoon."

"Your letter," I began—but I did not know how to proceed. This was a different Jo, neither welcoming nor in the grip of her own headstrong emotions. When had she ever rested?

"Oh, that! My mother's foolishness, nothing more. I will tell you about it later." At that her mouth turned up at the corners, more rictus than smile. It was ghastly to see. Still, she took my hand. "I will tell you, Caroline," she repeated. "Once I feel restored to myself. I promise."

"You know I am here for you," I said, squeezing her hand. "Whatever is the matter—whatever has happened—between ourselves we can solve it, like we always do."

There was a moment, then, when her lips parted, when I felt her about to embrace me and confess all ... but then she drew back, still smiling that deathly smile. "I know," she said too-brightly. "But it is nothing, truly. A—a misunderstanding, nothing more. I will rest and then address it."

Should I have pressed her? Oh, I thought to do so, even after she closed the door in my face. But in truth I knew little of Jo's family and their circumstances, save what she had told me that longago night in Harkworth Hall. To pry now seemed like it might only upset her further. Surely she would make her way to me when she was ready.

I went back downstairs. Mr. Simmons readied the carriage and I pressed close to my father as we rode down to the village, where we stopped for a little while before turning back. He no longer felt well enough to sit in the inn as he used to, but still many came out to greet him and shake his hand. The way his eyes lit up, the newfound vigor in his voice, distracted me from my concerns for Jo.

We returned in the afternoon, just as the air was turning chill. It was only as I was undoing my cloak that I remembered Mr. Smith's letter was in my pocket. Here was an excuse to talk to Jo, even if just to distract her as the ride had distracted me.

But when I went to her room, I found the door ajar, the bedcovers hastily dragged back into place, the fire banked in the hearth.

Jo was gone.

Dear Misses Chase and Daniels—

We have found a painting that bears a striking resemblance to the one you described in Thomas Masterson's hallway, in the bedroom of a lord we suspect was murdered. It would be of great help if you could come to London and confirm this is the same work. We would of course provide your transportation and lodging for this inspection, and for any further assistance you might be able to provide. I have instructed Mr. Windham to return to London by way of your village, to either assist you in your journey south or to apologize on my behalf for disturbing your tranquility.

Your obliged, &c.,
J. Smith

CHAPTER II

A Quiet House

*J*n Jo's absence it was as if the air had left the house, making the empty rooms oppressive, even stifling. I told my father and the Simmonses that Jo had been called away unexpectedly; I tried to believe my own words. They were true in a sense, but the suddenness of her departure, how she had shied away from me—it was not the woman I knew, the one I had come to love and trust with my life.

On the pretext of airing out her room I looked more carefully at what she had left behind. She had taken a dress in addition to a change of linen, rather than a second suit. Though I told myself I was being foolish, the choice struck me as ominous. She still wore dresses at times, though with increasing rarity, and when she did she was such a picture of awkwardness that my heart would go out to her. That she would choose the hated garment now—! But perhaps it was her mother's wish, and who would not endure such awkwardness for a parent, no matter how fraught the relationship?

Her things were in typical disarray, papers and books left where she dropped them, a pair of scuffed shoes forgotten in the corner. I told myself I would not pry, keeping my eyes averted as I tidied the papers on her desk—and there was no point in my doing so, for even my partial glimpse told me they were mostly legal documents. Only as I set the stacks neatly side by side did I see the note that had fallen among them, probably as she snatched up something in her haste, with my name at the top in her elegant, rounded script.

I must speak with my sister. Will write more from London and return as soon as I can. I—

But the last was a smudge, so that I could not even tell if she had meant to write more, or just dropped her pen.

A reasonable enough missive, and perhaps that was why it bothered me. The Jo I knew either discussed every detail before arriving at a decision, or rashly jumped into a situation; there was no middle ground. This uncertainty felt like a Jo torn between her two selves—and without my steadying influence, where would her actions take her?

I kept up my appearance of normalcy for supper, but there was no avoiding how somber the table was. Nor could I fail to notice how the others kept giving me surreptitious glances, as if trying to ascertain the degree of my masquerade. We dined together now, but it felt as if we were four strangers, so halting was our conversation. At last my father leaned over and murmured something to Mr. Simmons, who nodded.

"Miss," he said carefully, "if there's something afoot, you can go after her, you know. Jane and I can look after your father."

Mrs. Simmons took that moment to rise and carve more meat at the sideboard.

"Afoot? There's nothing afoot," I said, trying to keep my tone light. "Jo has some family business, as I said."

"Smith," my father said, jabbing his knife in the direction of my lap, where the letter still sat in my pocket.

I frowned at this—how had he seen the letter? "He merely sent us news. There is nothing requiring my attention."

"Begging your pardon, Miss, but Miss Chase might." Mrs. Simmons slapped a piece of meat on my plate as she spoke, the sound loud in the room. Her acceptance of Jo had taken the shape of a grudging truce, and I suspected it pained her to advocate for Jo now. "She was distraught when she left today, almost as bad as when they pulled her ashore at Medby. Perhaps there was a death in the family," she added reflectively.

I must speak to my sister. I shook my head. "I suspect it may be a more delicate matter," I said. Jo's sister had fallen under the sway of an evil man once before. If it had happened again … but why not tell me? She had told me everything before now.

Or so I thought.

"If you want to go to London—" Mr. Simmons began, but I held up a hand before he could finish.

"Jo will be fine. I spoke with her before she left and she assured me all will be explained on her return." I made myself smile as I spoke. The memory of Jo's strained expression rose before me, though I forced it aside. "She will be home before we've had time to miss her," I added, and cut into my meat before they could press the matter further.

But I was already missing her.

That night Mr. Simmons got my father settled in bed and then I sat with him, reading patiently from one of his favorites, though his choice seemed a continuation of the day's unsettling events:

Now entertain conjecture of a time
When creeping murmur and the poring dark
Fills the wide vessel of the universe.

He stopped me, however, and gestured for his pen and paper. The injuries he had sustained the previous year inhibited his speech, but over time he had regained enough coordination to write, and often turned to paper to express more complicated thoughts. Jo and I had resurrected an old lap desk from the attic, cleaning it and outfitting it with a sturdy pen and a stack of foolscap. Though I was generally overjoyed that my father had regained a means of communication, I found myself dreading the import now. The Simmonses might be polite enough to not remark on my forced good humor, but my father would not be so circumspect.

At last he handed me the paper, the ink still glistening in the spattered, cobwebby hand he now wrote in:

You should not fear London. You are capable. Look at all you did in Medby. If England needs you, you must answer. I have all confidence for your success.

I read it over a second time, a dozen thoughts fighting for utterance. That he could at once see, and yet not see—! Did he think Jo had gone to Mr. Smith and I had lingered from cowardice? Did he not believe me when I spoke of her family obligation?

Did he not understand that it was my very strength that frightened me, when it had run so easily to murder?

Oh, at any other time knowing he had such faith in me would have warmed me like sunshine. Now it seemed a cold, mocking thing, on a par with Jo's empty bedroom.

"Mr. Smith merely said a—a painting we had seen in Medby has been found," I admitted. "He wants us to confirm it is the same picture."

Unbidden, the memory rose before me: of climbing the stairs to Thomas Masterson's office, of pausing before that family portrait, and how the canvas had seemed to *move* of its own accord …

My father simply looked at me, waiting. I sighed then. "And Jo never saw his letter. I hadn't even told her of its arrival."

His eyebrows raised, but still he waited. Oh, he knew me too well! "She received a letter from her family. She would not tell me what it said, only that she was going to rest and think on her reply while we went out in the carriage. When we returned she was gone. She left a note but it only said she must speak to her sister. She took a, a *dress*, and I cannot understand …" I took a breath to calm the shudder in my voice. "I cannot understand why she would not speak to me. We have always discussed everything—or so I thought. I certainly have no secrets from her, I've told her things even when I was ashamed, or frightened, or—"

My father leaned forward and hugged me awkwardly, the lap desk poking painfully in my stomach. I kissed his cheek and moved the desk aside, though I kept a grip on his hand, relishing the comfort it gave me.

"Protecting you?" he offered, wiping at a tear winding down my cheek.

"But from what? She told me of her sister's near-elopement with Edward Masterson, she told me how she pretended to be her own brother to save her family from debt." I was biting my lip in my consternation. "What did she think I could not understand?"

"Ask her," my father said.

I nodded heavily. "In the morning. I'm too distraught to write now—"

He was shaking his head. "Ask," he said, tapping his mouth. "Go to London."

"But—that's absurd." I stared at him. "To go so far, just to find out what she will probably tell me in a letter?" *To leave you*, I added silently.

"Smith needs you." He nodded again at my lap. "Could be—" He broke off, struggling to speak. He started to reach for the lap desk, but instead said, "Exact words."

Unwillingly I took out Mr. Smith's letter and read it to him, wincing at how vigorously he nodded at each phrase. "A crime," he said as soon as I finished. "More treason."

"It's highly unlikely to be the same painting," I replied, a little irritated. "A family portrait, under a tree? There must be dozens such in London alone. And even if it was Thomas Masterson's," I continued as he started to speak, "it was probably bought at some market after being stolen in Medby. The Mastersons are both dead. There is nothing more for us to do."

My father, however, was looking at me with a kind of bemused frustration I remembered well from childhood, especially when I was arguing for more sweets. "London," he said, holding up two fingers. "Two birds."

I bit my lip again. *Stop chewing those lovely lips*, Jo whispered in my mind, and my stomach knotted anew. Something was wrong, I could not deny my instinct. But to leave my father—

"Take Missus Simmons," he said then.

"Certainly not," I replied hotly. Too often Mr. Simmons was out of the house, seeing to the land and its upkeep. What if something happened to my father and he was all alone? "Mister Windham will convey me to London. The Simmonses both stay," I said to his mulish expression, "or I do."

Still scowling, my father nodded once, then leaned back against the pillows as if suddenly exhausted. Swiftly, I put away the desk and book, then settled him more comfortably. "We will speak of it again in the morning," I said, kissing his cheek once again, then went about extinguishing the candles.

As I bent to put out the last, however, I thought I saw a gleam of tears in his eyes. Startled, I raised the candle, but he had shut them completely, and I did not want to risk awakening him. That shimmering reflection, however, lingered in my mind for some time, a note of concern amidst all my roiling emotions as I grappled with the realization that, despite my resistance, I was entering Mr. Smith's dark agenda once more.

CHAPTER III

Mr. Windham

I set myself to answering Mr. Smith in the morning—
and here I faltered, for I knew not what to say. Would
Jo have encountered him by the time my letter arrived?
Might she turn to him, an older friend, before me? Yet to
ask him about her might impinge on her privacy. I fretted
until I thought my heart would burst, and then I simply said
I was coming, and handed the missive to Mr. Simmons to
post before I could start worrying again.

The afternoon post contained a note from Mr. Windham,
very hurried, with the import that he was nearly upon us.
I spent the evening packing and repacking, for I knew not
the shape of my journey. Was I packing for two weeks, or
a month, or longer? The business with the painting was a
matter of minutes, but what if Jo needed aid? What if she
refused to see me? Or perhaps she wasn't even in London—
perhaps her sister was elsewhere, and Jo had rushed to her
side. Would I press on to find her, or return home to wait
for her? There were no answers to any of my questions, and
I became aware that my fears for her were also mingled with
anger, at being so swiftly abandoned without explanation.

The day of Mr. Windham's arrival dawned cool and

crisp—and punctuated by a deep cough emanating from my father's bedroom. I sat up in bed, listening with a sinking heart: how could I leave him now? In his weakened state, every cough, every fever, would prostrate him, and I knew it was only a matter of time before he fell ill and did not recover.

The thought of him passing while I was far away—but no, I could not bear to think of it. He would not. He would not.

Slowly I began to dress, eyeing my packed satchel. And if I did not go to Mr. Smith now, after giving my word? His money paid for the upkeep of our house, his physician in Medby had watched over my father for those last weeks while we waited for the roads to clear. I knew little of him save that he served our king and could seemingly bring down ministers. What might he do, what could he do, if I changed my mind and did not come?

My father coughed again and I reached for my satchel to unpack it, only to be interrupted by a swift knock and Mrs. Simmons peeking inside. "Aha!" she said when she saw me. "I knew it! Don't you dare unpack, Miss."

"Missus Simmons," I began, but she shook her head.

"Your father sent me to tell you that. There's no fever, only a bit of damp in his lungs. He'll stay in bed today and get some good broth in him, and I'll make him a tisane to help clear it out. There's nothing for you to do, so you can go to London."

"But—" I began again, but she bustled over and took the satchel from me. At my stricken expression, however, she put it down and laid her hands on my arms.

"You cannot spend all your life fussing over him," she said

more quietly. "It won't change the outcome, Miss. When God calls him, He won't wait, the better for you to have a few more days. Don't sacrifice the life ahead of you for the inevitable."

Tears rushed to my eyes at her words. I was fumbling to form my own ... but just then Mr. Simmons called upstairs, saying that Mr. Windham had arrived. With an encouraging hug and a peck on my cheek Mrs. Simmons caught up my satchel and fled with it, and I was left alone to compose myself. Leaving again. Unlike our journey to Medby, I felt certain I would return. It was the possible shape of my homecoming that filled me with unease. To return alone, to spend my days losing everything I held dear—my father, my home, *Jo*—it seemed as horrifying a prospect as any of Mr. Smith's assignments.

I looked at myself in the mirror, raising my chin as I did so. *You've got that doing look about you*, Jo laughed in my mind. *What project are you tackling now?*

"The project of bringing you home," I replied aloud.

So fortified, I strode down the stairs, making myself smile at the sight of Mr. Windham conversing with Mr. Simmons. His familiar, ruddy face brought back memories of Medby in a rush. Then I had felt so close to Jo, and so far from myself; now all was terribly reversed. Still, I embraced him warmly. His teaching and his actions had saved our lives, and I took comfort in knowing I was not completely alone.

"Miss Daniels," he said with a smile when we drew apart. "It has been far too long. You've been keeping up your exercises, I hope?"

"A little," I parried. My defense lessons with Mr. Windham seemed a lifetime ago, yet I suspected I would never truly forget them, having put them to such use in the interim.

"Any woman should know enough to protect both purse and person. If I had my way, they would teach it in the schools—but you have heard me discourse on the topic before," he added swiftly. "Mister Simmons has explained that it is you and I to London. The sooner we go, the sooner we can return."

"Agreed," I said, "and I am already packed."

"And I took the liberty of booking two rooms on the fastest ship out of Newcastle," he said with approval. "Only may I see your father before we go? It's been far too long since I enjoyed his company."

The thought of a boat journey made me flinch, but I masked my reaction. The quicker to London, the quicker to Jo. "But of course," I replied, keeping my tone light. "He has missed you in turn, Mister Windham. Only take care that he does not question you too closely on the state of England. He's supposed to avoid agitation."

"Alas, that would take far too long to recount, if we're to get a start today. I will keep it brief and calm." With a slight bow he went upstairs. A moment later, I heard my father greet him heartily.

"A fine gentleman," Mr. Simmons said, but as he spoke I looked past him to the front, where the carriage was already hitched and waiting.

"So soon," I whispered.

"Soon? It's well into morning, Miss, and it'll be a hard

road to Newcastle." Mr. Simmons laid a hand on my arm, just as his wife had done. "Now, don't you fret. We will look after your father, and the doctor is a short ride away."

"I've already given her a talking to," Mrs. Simmons put in, holding out my cloak and bonnet.

"You have Mister Smith's address?" I asked, looking from one to the other.

"We both have it," Mrs. Simmons confirmed. "I will write in a day or two, and let you know all that's happened."

"Which may even amount to a whole three lines," Mr. Simmons teased. "You just make sure you bring back some new reading for your father, he'll be peevish by the time you return."

"I will," I said, and then I realized there was nothing more to say. "I will," I repeated. "Only I should say good-bye."

Upstairs I found Mr. Windham sitting on the edge of my father's bed, leaning forward to hear his words and nodding. My father looked tired and anxious, and Mr. Windham's expression was serious. I felt a pang, studying them; I knew that Mr. Windham was the kind of man my father had hoped for in a son-in-law. Did my father understand, truly understand, why I would never marry? I could not say.

Brave girl, he had said in Medby. *Mine.* Let him think of me like that, and nothing more; let him remember me—

But I was being foolish. It was as the Simmonses had said: the worst I would come back to would be a grumpy, neglected Theophilus Daniels. Better for me to focus on what lay ahead—

The life ahead of you—

And figuring out what I would do if—*when*—I saw Jo again.

I cleared my throat and the two men looked up, both with such guilty expressions that I found myself frowning in turn. "What are you two plotting?" I asked.

"Nothing," my father retorted, while Mr. Windham said more placidly, "Nothing more than a father's natural concerns for his daughter, which of course I take as seriously as he."

"And you have taught me accordingly," I replied.

"A point I have reminded your father of. You handle yourself well, and you will have me to ensure you encounter no difficulties, so there is no cause for worry." He clasped my father's hands. "She will be back before you know it," he said, and took his leave of us.

Before the door had closed completely I found myself speaking in a rush. "I will of course bring back all the papers, from the Continent as well. And new poetry, several volumes if we can afford it, and that philosophe the vicar spoke of—Voltaire, wasn't it—"

"Caroline," my father said.

His voice brought me up short. We looked at each other and then I went and hugged him. "I am well," he said into my hair, though his voice was gravelly. "Only—home soon, yes?"

"Yes," I breathed.

"Good girl." He held me a moment longer, then released

me. We took a look at each other, and we each drew out our handkerchief for the other's eyes; I laughed then as we dabbed in an easier silence.

"I am sorry," he said.

"For what? You didn't send Jo away—"

"The house." He swallowed. "Entailment. Never thought…" He shook his head. "Never thought," he said more softly.

Of course he had not thought. He had believed I would be like any other woman: long married by now, with a home elsewhere. I patted his hand, alarmed to see it trembling. "Jo will figure something out," I said, trying to sound as reassuring as possible. "She may have a solution already, with her father's friends to hand. And if not …" I looked around, then shrugged. "What does it matter where we are, as long as we're together?"

He hugged me again, more tightly this time, and I laughed when he rocked us both from side to side.

"Go on, then," he said, his voice thick as he released me. When I was halfway to the door he added with vigor, "And books!"

"And books," I agreed, laughing again. He was smiling when I closed the door between us. That the latch sounded strangely final, I did not let myself dwell on.

We dined late that evening in a pleasant inn, introducing ourselves as cousins on our way to visit family. Throughout this first day of our journey, Mr. Windham had kept the conversation light and let me doze in the rare stretches when the road smoothed out. Only now, with full bellies, the last of the burgundy, and the warmth of the dining room fire upon us, did he ask, "Will Miss Chase be joining us in London?"

I started to bite my lip but caught myself. I was giving myself away. It was one thing to react thoughtlessly in the safety of my home, but I was not home anymore. No matter how innocuous the summons seemed, Mr. Smith's world was one of violence and death, and I was in his world now.

"I don't know," I admitted. "She went to visit her sister."

"About the wedding, I suppose?"

The word *wedding* made me start, and he looked startled in turn. "I thought you knew," he said apologetically, "but perhaps the news hadn't traveled yet." He hesitated, but I met his gaze levelly. "It is the talk of London. The daughter of a barrister, one of dubious reputation no less, snaring a nobleman. He's the firstborn son of Viscount Pestell. His fortune will be substantial, and he has the ambition to match."

"I—I see." I did not know whether to be relieved or more frightened. My first thought had been for Jo, that he spoke of some terrible coercion. But an ambitious nobleman might not look kindly upon a sister-in-law who dressed in breeches and fought both men and monsters—even if her actions bore a royal seal of approval. "It sounds a brilliant match," I added weakly.

"It is for the sister—they say it may even be for love. Apparently he's as smitten as she is."

"For her sister, but not for Jo," I said.

Mr. Windham shook his head. "I cannot see how it would be. He has political ambitions; he needs a family that is the picture of respectability. A sister-in-law with outlandish habits would hamstring him."

"She masqueraded at the behest of our king." I kept my voice low, but I was starting to feel a rising anger now, as if it were not Mr. Windham sitting across from me but this mysterious son. It wasn't quite the whole truth—she had already adopted the guise when Mr. Smith approached her, to keep control of her late father's income—but I felt, instinctively, how precarious her position was.

"But she cannot say so," Mr. Windham replied. He looked around the empty dining room, then leaned across the table. "Mister Smith works at the behest of the Crown, it is true. But he works in secret, Miss Daniels. It is what gives him, and those he employs, the leeway to do what must be done. Should Miss Chase try to bring it to light she will find herself without friends; should she press the matter, she might find herself placed where she cannot be heard."

The room seemed to darken as he spoke, and my body went cold despite the fire. I wanted nothing more than to fly to her, shake her, make her speak to me: *what are you doing, what is happening, why did you go back?*

"And I am painting a dire picture, when it may be of no consequence," he amended, touching my hand. "Perhaps she is simply helping her sister with preparations, nothing more."

"No, there is something more," I replied grimly, "and your picture is indeed dire. Whatever her situation? She has *me*, Mister Windham. And I will not let anything happen to her."

At my resolute tone he smiled then and raised his glass. "She has *us*, Miss Daniels," he said.

I raised my own. The rich burgundy heated my cold belly, fuel for a blossoming fire. If she thought to fight her own battles—if she thought to protect *me*—Joanna Chase was sorely mistaken. We were partners, whether she wanted one or not, and I would be damned before I let anyone harm her.

CHAPTER IV

Mr. Smith

*J*had been to London once before, when I was much younger. It was not long after my mother had died. My father said only that he had family business, which I assumed had to do with her passing. Certainly, we had no other family, save the distant cousin who was poised to inherit our house. Now I wondered just what he had meant by *business*. I thought I knew his dealings inside and out, having kept our books for so long, but I had not known about the entailment, nor did I know anything of my mother's family. Even then, it had struck me as odd for him to go so far, much less bring his young daughter with him. Surely a lawyer could have made the journey to us, or sent an agent? But perhaps he had needed to escape the house, so recently the scene of his grief. Perhaps he had needed us both to escape.

As Jo had perhaps escaped her family for a time?

But all my musings on her led to darkness, so instead I took to pacing the deck of our battered collier, the better to observe London as we finally arrived. Young Caroline had been both entranced and terrified by the city, awash in its roaring energy even as her father tried to shelter her from the crudeness of its inhabitants. It was so vast, so overwhelming after life in our little village. Had he not regaled me with tales of London, I might have begged to go home that very first day. So many people, of every hue and appearance—! I had not understood that there were so many souls in the world, and as I looked at each, dark and pale, rich and poor, for the first time I had a glimmer of comprehension at the size of the globe, and my own ant-sized role in it.

As much as I had seen and done since then, I still felt a shiver of awe as we drew closer to the smudge of buildings and the ship-choked Thames running between. The rhythmic splashing of waves that had marked our journey was slowly drowned out by a mindless roar, equal parts voices and movement and the rush of water beneath London Bridge, where the river was throttled into rapids. The sight of the bridge reminded me that the new bridge at Westminster was reportedly finished at last. I made an inward note to buy my father an etching if I chanced upon one.

We docked close to the bridge. I was eager to be off the ship, for the last few days had been difficult, the rough seas conspiring with my memories of the *Leviathan* to keep me from sleeping at all. Thankfully, Mr. Windham had our luggage ready and a hansom summoned and waiting by the time I stepped gratefully onto the solid, unmoving land.

It was late morning when we set out for Mr. Smith's house, and the streets were thronging. I had thought London would feel more manageable for a grown woman than a child. If anything, however, it felt much more chaotic. My father had opined a few times that London seemed to be swelling with people, and it certainly felt more populous. The streets were alive with languages utterly unknown to me, accents I could in no way place, costumes that bore little resemblance to my own plain dress—though whether from foreign custom or fashion I often couldn't say. I was too tired to formulate questions for Mr. Windham; instead I gave myself over to looking, drinking in the passing streets as we lurched and rattled forward. Not just any city, but Jo's home, the place that had shaped her. I tried to see her as a little girl, walking with her family; I tried to see her as a young woman donning her first suit and stepping out into this genteel chaos, where probably not a single person paid her any mind. What a moment it must have been—the sudden freedom, the sudden possibilities—and perhaps, too, the sense of being herself, truly, at last.

"Nearly there," Mr. Windham said, and I roused myself enough to nod at him. He smiled sympathetically. "You are quite worn out. I think we can persuade Mister Smith to let you rest before we venture forth again—?"

But I was shaking my head. "No," I said. "Let us be done with it. I want to see to Jo as soon as possible."

He seemed about to argue, but then he, too, peeked out the window and gave a decisive nod. "We are here," he said.

I looked in the direction he indicated. It may have been my exhaustion, but I felt bewildered. I cannot say what exactly I had expected as the residence of my mysterious employer. A hovel in some uncouth neighborhood, perhaps, the better to darkly plot for His Majesty; or the calm of some hidden office in Parliament, overseeing espionage and murder from behind a plain door; or even a second life as something both ordinary and exemplary in order to better hide his actions.

What I had never imagined was that I would find him in a large, fashionable house in St. James' Square, shoulder to shoulder with all manner of wealthy, dignified families. Yet it was here the carriage halted, exactly in front of clean white steps leading up to a pedimented door. Flowers were budding in the window boxes, and at the very top of the four stories, a bright muslin curtain was blowing out an open window. It was precisely the abode of a noble family, and precisely not what I envisioned for a man who thwarted treasonous plots and hunted sea monsters.

Mr. Windham disembarked and helped me out, while directing our driver to bring our meager luggage. Again I paused, taking in the pretty square and the even rows of houses that framed it. Down the street a pale, elegant woman was being helped into a chaise by an equally pale and elegant gentleman, while a small, dark-skinned child held up the hem of her skirts. I had been to balls and assemblies with local nobility up north, but never had I seen such a strange display before, from the oversized, exotic feathers on the woman's hat to the jewels around her neck, to the gentleman's ornately embroidered coat, and especially that too-young brown face gazing at the ground. His livery was as fine as the driver's, and he was swung up beside the lady. As he settled himself, the gentleman stroked the boy's hair. Only then did the lady nod in my direction, and I realized that in my exhausted state I had been staring. Quickly, I curtseyed and looked away, feeling shabby and ashamed and queer all at once, as if I were in a foreign land. My father was a gentleman, but clearly a different breed of such. It was with relief that Mr. Windham took my arm and guided me inside.

In the entrance hall we were greeted by a burly servant, his face deeply tanned, so muscular and robust he seemed to strain his jacket, his grey wig absurdly curled for his large features. "Good to see you, Charlie," Mr. Windham said. "This is Miss Caroline Daniels."

"Mister Windham." The men shook hands vigorously, and then Charlie executed an awkward bow. "And Miss. He's expecting you." There was a smothered accent to his voice, though I could not quite place it. His awkward manners told me he had not been born to his profession. He would probably ruin any garment he pressed, but he could put the fear of God into a man.

We were shown into a study, its curtains opened to reveal a neat garden behind the house. It should have been a pleasant, airy space, with its high ceilings, elegant moldings and shelves of bound tomes, but instead it looked as if a whirlwind had passed through. Desk, chairs, and floor were covered with papers, from small notes to large, curling maps. Some of the papers were neatly inscribed and bore officious seals, others were hasty things, with blotches and crossed-out words. In the midst of it all stood Mr. Smith, sunlight dappling the dark olive of his skin, frowning as he held a letter up to read it. He glanced at us and his frown deepened. "Where's Chase?" he demanded.

"Hullo to you too," Mr. Windham retorted. He stepped carefully over the papers, then lifted a stack of books off a chair and gestured me to it.

I sat down and arranged myself before replying. "She has a family matter," I said. "You will have to make do with me."

"She's not gone home?" He looked at me over his spectacles, his brown eyes piercing.

"And what if she has?"

"Then she's a fool," he said. "Pestell isn't marrying her sister for love, he's buying a career. Few noblemen have the mercantile connections that Matthew Chase had. It will give him an advantage in Parliament, especially in matters of trade." Mr. Smith shook his head. "He wants those connections and he wants a pretty wife to parade about. He won't tolerate a tribade sister flouncing about in men's clothes."

"Jo never flounces," I snapped.

He snorted at that, but he laid the letter atop another precarious stack and held out his hand to me. "And I've been remiss. I do appreciate you coming, Miss Daniels. Your father is well, I hope?"

"Well enough." I shook his hand. "Though I hope to make this a short visit."

"And it should be. I strongly suggest you take Miss Chase back with you, before Pestell tries to exert himself." He looked around. "I'll just fetch my coat and we can go."

"What do you mean, exert himself—" I began, only to be interrupted in turn as a far door opened and a tall, powdered man in a silken banyan half-entered, holding an overcoat before him.

"Looking for this?" he asked lightly.

The question provoked the most remarkable reaction. All of Mr. Smith's poise vanished; he looked almost embarrassed, yet there was a little smile curling up his mouth. He quickly crossed the room and took the coat, whispering in the man's ear as he did so. There was, apparently, to be no introductions.

Beside me, Mr. Windham cleared his throat. "What he means, Miss Daniels, is that Pestell might want assurances."

"Assurances." I looked up at him, frowning. "What do you mean, assurances?"

He hesitated, clearly wanting Mr. Smith to speak, but the latter was still in whispered conference, the overcoat tangled between them. "I mean a—a guarantee, of behavior."

"A guarantee?" I twisted in my seat fully. "What kind of guarantee? And what kind of behavior?"

"Pestell might make it a condition of the marriage," Mr. Smith said, drawing on his coat as he returned to us. "That Miss Chase return to the fold, so to speak. Dress properly, act the part of a spinster sister, perhaps even marry. Respectability can be everything, Miss Daniels; more than one career has foundered on the rocks of the mildest scandal."

I gaped at them both. "And if she doesn't agree to his assurances?"

The two men exchanged looks. "Just take her back north, Miss Daniels," Mr. Smith said. "After you've taken care of my little chore, of course. Shall we?"

I was shaking my head. All through our journey I had carried within my belly a knot of worry for Jo and now that knot had flowered into panic. "I need to see Jo first," I said. When Mr. Smith's expression became grim I pressed, "It is to both our benefits. She may have seen some detail in the painting that I missed, she may be able to identify it with greater certainty. It won't take but a moment—"

We were interrupted by the main door swinging wildly open. Charlie stood there, his wig askew, a goggle-eyed boy crowding in behind him. "Begging your pardon, sir," he said, "but there's been another one."

CHAPTER V

The Second Murder

*O*nce again we were lurching through London's crowded streets. The noonday sun washed the landscape with yellow, every road choked with horses and carriages, sedan chairs and carts. Yet it all seemed to be happening at a remove, for my attention was on greater matters: that I was moving away from the woman I loved and towards violence once more. Every moment felt precious, every street we traversed seemed to count down to a terrible fate for us both. To choose her family would be to deny her very self; to choose me might mean giving up family and name alike. We might even have to flee England—

What would become of my father—

Mr. Windham touched my arm, and I realized Mr. Smith had been speaking. "Pardon?"

"I was saying that there is no need for you to remain after you view the room, Miss Daniels," he repeated. "The word is that the circumstances are the same as Lord Otterburn: windows and door locked from within, and the only recent change the acquisition of a large painting fitting the description of Masterson's. All I need from you is to tell me if the painting is indeed the one you saw."

"But there cannot be two paintings," I replied. "If the painting in question was in Lord Otterburn's room, how has it come to be here?"

"A very good question. I've sent Charlie to ensure that my instructions were obeyed and the room is still sealed. We may be looking at copies of the original, but if so, that makes their role more pointed, for they are now a direct link between two murders."

"Was he on the list?" Mr. Windham asked.

Mr. Smith nodded, explaining to me, "Though we arrested a few of the Mastersons' inner circle, there were nine men in the brothers' books whose involvement we could not prove. Each told us they thought they were speculating on a new trade route, not supporting a coup." He snorted. "Nine educated men, all known for their business acumen. Yet I'm to believe they were rooked by some vague trade scheme?"

"You should warn them," I said. "If someone is murdering the list, they must be told at once."

"And I will—once I am certain the Mastersons are the link." He smiled at my consternation. "If it turns out that I worried them unnecessarily I will discredit both myself and His Majesty for employing me—and perhaps create more openings for future plots. Powerful men hate to be disturbed, Miss Daniels."

"So you would put their lives at risk merely to avoid a dressing-down?" I retorted.

"Not completely at risk—after all, you are here now. Certainty is nearly to hand, and if the painting is indeed a link, I will raise the alarm at once."

He made to pat my hand, but I drew it away. There was a casualness in Mr. Smith's tone that rankled. The Caroline of a year ago might have missed it, but I knew now what it meant to kill a man, and to watch many other poor souls die in terrible circumstances. A year ago, too, I might have endorsed an argument that put the security of England before a half-dozen lives, yet now I could not feel so certain. Or perhaps it was merely a childish disappointment, that our kingdom was no ideal of government, but survived on deceit and subterfuge.

The bustle of London was giving way to countryside, with open fields and copses of trees between the houses. Now the carriage slowed, then worked its way down a raked drive. I leaned over Mr. Windham to peer at the house—but no, *house* was too poor a word for our destination. It was a magnificent hall, though narrower than the halls of the North, of four tall stories, with orchards and outbuildings aplenty.

"The latest investment of Sir Lewis Burton, recently deceased," Mr. Windham said in my ear. "A new breed of knight—the noble banker."

I nodded, though had I to guess I would have arrived at a similar formulation. The whole of the property seemed to say country gentleman, yet it would be a short drive to the banks of London. The ornamented entrance, the interlaced stone and brickwork, the precisely manicured gardens, all spoke of recent construction with no expense spared. Mr. Smith lowered a window, and the birdsong proved a melodic counterpoint to the distant murmur of the city.

That, and the sounds created by the several men pacing

around the house, some armed with rifles, two with dogs held close by lengths of rope. One waved to us as we halted before the broad wooden doors.

"Take her directly upstairs," Mr. Smith said to Mr. Windham. "If anyone asks, she is a nurse that I sent for."

The man appeared at his window, murmuring breathlessly and gesturing to the house. Mr. Windham opened the opposite door and disembarked, then helped me out. With a smile and a wave at the guards he took my arm and steered me inside. I removed my bonnet and smiled graciously at all and sundry, adopting what I hoped was a plausible expression for a young caregiver entering a house of grief.

Inside all was chaos. There were bewigged men in rich suits arguing with men of decidedly shabbier circumstances. We barely made it to the staircase for all the servants darting to and fro. One of the wealthy men caught my eye, and started to turn in our direction, but just at that moment a pained cry came from deeper in the house, followed by girlish shrieks of "Mama!" and childish sobbing. Everyone rushed towards a door, clearly the source of the commotion. In my ear Mr. Windham said, "quick now," and we darted up the stairs and around a curve so as to be out of sight. Here Mr. Windham paused, then caught a passing boy and said, "the room, lad," and we were off again, following the grubby, pointing hand down a narrower hall to an open door with a footman standing guard.

"No one comes in, sir," he began, but Mr. Windham reached into his pocket and drew out a piece of paper that he flashed before the man's face. In the dim light I doubted the footman could read it, but it had a large seal on the bottom that seemed to be enough. He stepped aside and Mr. Windham steered me through, halting me the moment we crossed the threshold.

"Look carefully now," he said in a low voice. "If it's like the previous murder, the door and windows were locked from within, and there will be no evidence of anyone entering or exiting."

"Was a weapon found?" I asked, matching his low tone, but he shook his head grimly.

It turned out to be a large bedroom—almost too large, and despite the spring warmth the room felt chilled. The fire was out in the grate, though it looked to have been lit the night before. Mr. Windham went to a desk and used the one burning candle to light several others. The bed linens were wrenched aside, there was a dark stain on the parquet, and splashes on the bed and a nearby slipper chair—

—and then I turned and looked at the space behind the open door, and saw what I had thought I would never see again.

The painting from Thomas Masterson's stairwell leaned against the wall, though a space had been prepared for its hanging. It was as I remembered it, even in size and scale: a large canvas showing a hillside with an oak tree, the sea in the distance; there was the father with the red rose in his lapel and the two Masterson boys. On the bottom of the frame had been affixed a simple brass plaque with a single word: *ARCADIA.*

The only difference was that the figure of the woman, who I had taken to be the mother of the Mastersons, was completely absent.

Astonished, I laid my bonnet aside and moved closer. Had the woman been painted over, surely there would have been additional pigment covering where she stood. Yet the surface was as even as if she had never existed at all. I moved to the side of the canvas, eyeing the surface, but there was nothing to indicate anything had been done to the painting.

A duplicate? Yet it was the spit of the Medby image in every other way.

"Bloody hell," Mr. Windham swore, coming up behind me. "Begging your pardon, Miss Daniels. But it matches Smith's description of the painting in Otterburn's house. Is it the same as Medby?"

"I'm not certain," I said, gesturing for the nearest candelabra. In Medby we had looked at the painting from the stairs, and in near darkness. Now, with the candles held close, I saw a shadow behind the boys, a soft yet distinct shape that might have been another figure, turned towards the sea.

"I would swear it was the same, yet there was a fourth figure," I said finally. "A woman, with the two boys."

"So someone could be making duplicates? A kind of warning, alluding to Masterson?"

"Perhaps," I said thoughtfully, looking up at him. "In every other way it looks identical. Yet I cannot see how the painter could have otherwise removed one figure and added another."

"Added one where?"

"Here, at the water." I turned back to the painting, raising my hand to where I had seen the shadow.

It was gone.

All sensation vanished from my body. I raised the candles again, but there was nothing save the limned hillside and the textured water beyond, all now shimmering, as I had seen that longago night—

Staring, I touched the canvas and, God help me, it was *warm,* warm and somehow *soft*—

"Damn it all," Mr. Smith swore behind us, and I jerked my hand away. My heart was racing, my breath a rasp in my ears.

Mr. Windham bent solicitously over me. "Miss Daniels? Miss Daniels, are you all right?"

"Touch it," I whispered.

He put his hand where mine had been, only to shake his head. "What am I feeling for?"

"Does it feel warm?"

Again he touched it, this time laying his palm over it. "No moreso than the surrounding area," he said.

"Is it the one from Medby?" Mr. Smith asked.

"Nearly, but there was a woman in that painting." I thought to say more about the shadow and the shimmering, but decided against it. What could they say, save that it was a trick of the light?

I wished then, desperately wished, that Jo would somehow appear. She would understand; she would believe me.

"Well, it's the spit of the one at Otterburn's house, right down to the missing woman." He pushed it forward to inspect the back of the canvas. "And without anything hidden, just as with its duplicate."

He drew Mr. Windham aside, speaking to him in a low voice. For my part I could not stop looking at the point where the shadowy figure had been. How had it vanished from sight? I touched the canvas again, but it was cool and firm. I brought my face within inches of the surface and in doing so saw a glimmer in the corner of my eye. When I turned my head it vanished; when I turned my gaze straight ahead once more and waited a few moments, it reappeared. Just the faintest hint of movement, as if a light was playing over that one tiny area.

"... take her there," Mr. Smith was saying, "and make your way to meet Morrow ..."

I raised my hand without moving my head until it hovered over the glimmer. Slowly, carefully, I brought my fingertips down upon it. Again, I felt warmth, and a soft, damp texture. I pressed and the surface *yielded*. It felt like pushing into warm mud—

There was a commotion outside the room, a cacophony of voices and thudding footsteps racing towards us. Mr. Smith exhaled and whispered something to Mr. Windham, who pulled me back from the painting. Before I could ask what was wrong, a woman entered, her stout form a mass of damask and lace, her blond hair unpinned and her unpainted face ravaged with grief. She stared at Mr. Windham and I as if we were unusual animals, and then she looked at Mr. Smith with utter loathing. "This is what will bring justice for my husband?" she demanded, her voice hoarse. Her skirts were fluttering, as if she were shaking beneath them. "This is how you protect England? With women and old men?"

"I beg your pardon," Mr. Windham said sharply, while Mr. Smith bowed deeply and said, "Mister Windham is a former intelligence officer, Lady Burton. I have asked his advice on the matter." He glanced at me. "His cousin is a nurse," he added.

"Advice for what? We know what this is!" She looked at each of us with wild, reddened eyes. "There is a murderer loose out there! Why aren't you combing the streets, why haven't you raised the alarm?"

Mr. Smith exhaled. "Someone find the butler—" he began, but I stepped forward.

"You've had a terrible shock," I said soothingly, taking her arm. "Why don't we sit somewhere? Is there a couch nearby, some brandy? You look terribly pale." Before Mr. Smith could object, I steered her towards the door. She was indeed trembling as I had thought. "We should not have come now," I continued in the same soothing tones. "We should not have intruded on your grief."

Gently, I led her into the hallway. A quick question to the footman pointed me in the direction of a little boudoir with a chaise in it. As I settled her on the chaise she managed a weak smile. "You are a kind girl," she rasped. When the footman reappeared with a large brandy she took it in both hands, like a child. "That Smith is so terrible," she added in a sodden voice. "Such an ugly little man."

I bit back my retort at this. "My lady," I began as she took a long swallow. "Mister Smith will bring the culprit to justice, I am certain of it. Once we ascertain the identity of the painter—"

"Oh, that painting!" she cried. "What does it matter? He bought the wretched thing as an act of charity, nothing more. He never could say no to a pretty face." She leaned forward, fixing me with her swollen eyes. "You can tell your *Mister* Smith that paint does not kill people. *Murderers* kill people. He should be going to the places where they congregate, not asking to see receipts for a painting."

"Cousin." We both turned to see Mr. Windham at the door, holding my bonnet. "He thanks you for your assistance and says I am to bring you where you like—and rest assured, Lady Burton, we will find this Loveless fellow. The artist," he explained.

"Oh yes, spend your time chasing Mister Loveless," Lady Burton exclaimed disgustedly. "Make that poor creature he married a widow—if he even married her. Those people never do." She began weeping.

"Miss Daniels," Mr. Windham said under his breath, but I held up my hand.

"That poor girl," I said to Lady Burton. "We could perhaps help her, if we could find her. Find her a better situation," I added when she frowned at me. "Something respectable. Sir Lewis would have wanted that, I'm sure."

At the latter Lady Burton sighed and leaned back on the chaise, massaging her temples. Mr. Windham laid his hand on my shoulder but again I held up my hand. We waited, silent, as her eyelids started to flutter closed. With a resigned shrug I began to rise—

—and then her eyes snapped open. "There was an agent," she whispered, looking at me with wet eyes. "A—a dealer, in paintings. We were to write to him if we had doubts about the provenance. His name was Mister Gribble."

CHAPTER VI

Miss Chase

"What will happen now?" I asked.

Across from me Mr. Windham stirred, then gave a little shrug. "He will warn the others and pursue this Loveless, I would think. Try to ascertain his connection to the Mastersons." At my consternation he leaned forward and patted my hand. "Don't worry about it. You have played your part, and we are grateful. You worry about Miss Chase."

I nodded, biting my lip as I gazed out the window. We were traversing London once more, on our way to the Chase house at last, yet now our afternoon encounter was tugging at my mind. The room had smelled faintly of blood, I realized. In the moment I had been fixed upon the painting, but now the smell came back to me. It reminded me of long ago when my mother had died, and I had snuck into that bedroom and seen all the blood—*her* blood. A stillborn brother and her own life lost in the process. Sometimes, in my darkest moods, I wondered if I had come to love women because of that day, because with a woman I would never have to fear such an agonizing death … but when I looked deep in myself I knew my desire had a deeper root than mere fear, that it came from the depths of my soul, that it was simply how I had been made.

Could Jo say the same? I believed so. Could she deny herself for the sake of her family? Marriage to a Viscount's son would mean the end of their precarity. If her sister loved the man that only made it the more blissful. She might not even see me—but oh! That I refused to believe. For months now we had lived side-by-side, we had survived encounters that were the stuff of broadsides and novels. I *knew* her now: even if her feelings for me had changed, I could not see Jo Chase taking up the mantle of reticent spinster. It was not for nothing that we both loved the story of Mary Read and Anne Bonny, the women pirates who had scandalized all of England.

Thinking of Jo provoked a physical ache of longing, so painful I nearly hugged myself. Mindful of Mr. Windham's presence, I distracted myself by trying to see Jo's London, matching her stories to the scenery. Perhaps that coffeeshop was one her father frequented, sometimes taking little Jo with him while he read the papers and discussed cases with his fellow lawyers. Perhaps that butcher's was where her mother shopped, not trusting the cook to choose the best cuts of meat. There were prettier windows too—a milliner, a haberdasher, a bakery with trays of cakes. Had these tempted Jo in her youth? A man was playing the fiddle mournfully at a corner, a few passerby forming a small audience—had Jo stopped to listen to him, or another? Among the people hurrying past were mothers with their daughters, each carrying baskets. It took little effort to see in them Jo and her mother and sister, running their daily errands or calling on friends.

When at last the chaise halted it was in sight of another

green square that I understood to be Bloomsbury. We were just around the corner from its elegant facades, in front of a tidy brick house with three stories, two windows wide. Her father, I knew, had wanted the proximity to both his clients and the wealthier barristers he aspired to become. Still, I was a little startled at the neighborhood—at one time Matthew Chase's career must have been quite profitable. Or perhaps he had overstretched himself in his attempt to move in higher circles, and compounded his financial woes.

Mr. Windham helped me out of the chaise, but when I held out my hand to shake his in farewell he nodded at the house. "I'll wait a few minutes," he said. "She may be out, and I would not want you to have to make your way alone."

At that I smiled. "I suspect I would be fine, thanks to your good tutelage."

"But why waste your skills on common or garden footpads?" He gestured to the horse and driver. "Especially when you have Smith's best chaise at your disposal."

"Only if you will not wait too long," I replied. When he assented, I turned and faced Jo's door. Aware of Mr. Windham watching, I climbed the steps without pause and knocked firmly, then pushed my trembling hands under my cloak. There were footsteps, the sound of a latch being undone, the door opened—

Revealing a slight, elderly butler looming in an impressive display of hauteur.

"Miss Daniels, to see Miss Chase," I said.

He frowned at me. "I did not know Miss Chase was expecting a visitor."

"I only just arrived in London," I explained. How to get him to fetch her? "My cousin and I were passing. I thought to visit briefly and invite her to dine with us."

His gaze passed over me. I was suddenly aware of my worn cloak and bonnet, the dress I had repaired and retrimmed just a few weeks ago, in a way I had not been even at Mr. Smith's. Still, after this lengthy perusal he gestured me inside. "You can wait in the study," he said, indicating a door on the right. "I will see if Miss Chase is receiving."

I stepped into the room he indicated and let out a small gasp of pleasure. It was no mere study; it was a library of remarkable size, every wall fitted with shelves to house the inordinate number of books. Nor was it mere display: the plump leather spines all showed degrees of wear, and the massive book on its own lectern was stuck with many pinned slips. A quick glance told me most of the books were legal works, and I had a vision of an older man with Jo's fierce grey eyes poring over them late into the night, the many tarnished lamps burning. Ink still dotted the surface of the empty desk tucked into a corner, and pins were still stuck in the arm of one of the low, comfortable chairs by the hearth. And what of young Joanna Chase, come to visit with her father, who she had so deeply cared for? Here, I suspected, were the seeds of her own clear reasoning and determination to fight, even when it meant resorting to violence.

I removed my bonnet only to catch sight of myself in a small mirror. Windswept and disheveled, it was a wonder I had been granted admittance. I peered more closely, trying to pat my hair into something passable. I licked my thumb and tried to remove the dirt from my face. She would think I had lost my senses, coming so far and turning up like this—

The door opened behind me and I spun about, only to find myself gaping at the younger woman who entered, so soft and lovely as to seem a vision. In Agnes Chase's face, her sister's angular features were rounded and full, her skin a milky white that knew nothing of long walks and riding. Blond hair, perfectly curled, replaced Jo's unruly brown waves. Her dress was exquisitely fitted, and a simple locket accented her slim, bare neck.

"Oh," she said, raising a hand to her mouth, so prettily as to almost seem affected. "I thought you were Lucy!"

I inclined my head. "My apologies, Miss Chase. I was hoping to see your sister."

At that her expression changed to grim displeasure. It sat ill on her girlish face. She carefully shut the door and I saw that her fine hands were trembling. When she turned back to me she stuck out her chin, a gesture so familiar my heart ached. "I know who you are," she said. "Joanna is not here, Miss—ah—"

"Daniels," I supplied.

"—and I'm afraid I must ask that you explain your relation to my sister."

"Pardon?"

"I must know, Miss Daniels. Who are you to Joanna?" She held herself upright, her hands now clasped before her, but I could see her slight frame was shaking and there was a gleam of tears in her eyes. "In what capacity has she been living with you?"

I hesitated, trying to weigh out my response—but I was keenly aware of Mr. Windham and the chaise, and was Jo truly not there, or was she in the depths of the house? "I think," I said carefully, "you should ask your sister that."

"Do you think I haven't tried?" She began pacing around the room, wringing her hands. "I cannot understand her, I cannot. She can come home now. She can come home and we can forget the whole terrible affair ever happened, she can be herself once more. Why won't she simply sign the papers? Why won't she be my sister again?"

The last came out as a cry. I gave her my handkerchief, which she snatched from me and used to violently dab at her eyes. "Perhaps because she never stopped being your sister," I offered.

"In breeches?" Agnes laughed bitterly. "With thieves, and murderers, and fallen women as her companions? Oh yes, she has been an *excellent* sister."

At the last she gave herself over to weeping, sinking into the nearest chair and crushing my handkerchief to her face. I let the *fallen women* pass, though I took a moment to calm my rush of anger before asking, "What papers?"

She took several shuddering breaths before gasping out, "He wants her assurances. Give up being Jonathan. Dress properly. Find a husband."

"And he would have this in writing?"

At that her gaze hardened. "There is nothing you can say that she has not already said. What cost is it to promise to be yourself? How is that an insult? It isn't even *about* her. It is about making sure that none of her acquaintances can use her past against us. It is a perfectly reasonable request."

And there were many arguments I wanted to raise to that, but not a one would have proved profitable. "Is there somewhere else she might be? Perhaps staying with one of her acquaintances?"

She blew her nose before replying. "She is probably at that rotten club of theirs," she said sulkily. "Seeing her *tailor* no doubt."

The word *tailor* was pronounced with such childish disgust that I nearly burst out laughing. "Heaven forbid she be fitted," I replied. "What is the name of this club?"

"Callisto House." The sulk deepened. "But do not ask me where it is. I shouldn't even know its name." She eyed me then, and a sly smile appeared on her face. "Why, do you like being fitted as well?"

I was already straightening my bonnet in the mirror. I glanced at her over my shoulder. "Now that is in poor taste, Miss Chase, especially for a future Lady." I walked to the door, adding, "You may keep the handkerchief."

Just as I began to open it, though, a cold hand seized my wrist. I looked down to see Agnes, leaning so far across as to nearly topple from the chair. "I love my sister, Miss Daniels," she said in a sodden voice. "And I love my fiancé. What would you do, if you were me?"

I looked at her for a long moment. As much child as woman, and what did she truly know of life? I bent down, lowering my voice to a whisper. "A person cannot survive with their choices taken from them, Miss Chase. It breaks their spirit." Gently I extracted my wrist from her grasp. "I will see myself out."

As the butler opened the door I felt a pang of relief at the sight of the chaise. I strode out with a nod and helped myself inside, grateful that Mr. Windham said nothing more than "where would you like to go now?"

"She is staying nearby, only I do not know the exact address," I said, taking the time to rearrange myself and thus avoid his gaze. I felt both frustrated and exhilarated in equal measure. She was gone, but she had not given in to them. She was choosing to be herself, with or without me. "It is called Callisto House."

Mr. Windham frowned at the name, then leaned forward and spoke in a low voice to the coachman. An animated conversation ensued, until at last he sat back, a hint of a smile on his face. "He will take us there," he explained, "though he wanted to be clear: it is a house for unnatural women, and not fit for a gentlewoman such as yourself."

At that I burst out laughing. All my worries, all my uncertainties, seemed to pour out of me. "Unnatural women?" I gasped, wiping at my damp eyes. "It sounds like home to me."

CHAPTER VII

Callisto House

This time my ride was short-lived; we had only pro-
gressed a few streets when traffic made our transit all
but impossible. It was all I could do to mask my frustration
and say, as lightly as possible, "I think I shall walk from here.
Can the coachman direct me?"

Mr. Windham did not argue as I had expected. He stepped
down from the chaise, looking in all directions, and then
nodded. "I have to agree with you, Miss Daniels. It seems an
unusually crowded market day, and I have an appointment
of my own to keep."

"Then it will benefit us both," I said with satisfaction, ad-
justing my cloak and bonnet.

He conferred at length with the coachman while I
twitched with impatience. At last he returned to me. "He
says go left around the market square, there—" He pointed
straight ahead. "—and keep going past the church that faces
the square, St. Paul's. You will know the house by sight."

"But how—?" My question, however, only garnered a
shrug. When I rose to disembark, he laid a hand on my arm,
then held out a folded knife to me.

"Take it," he said. "You should not be without protection.

Mister Smith's home is quite near, you can send for conveyance or Charlie at any time, but especially in this neighborhood a woman should take precautions."

I had thought myself done with knives, but Jo was close now, so close—! I took the blade and put it in my pocket. Mr. Windham helped me out, and then I shook his hand in farewell.

"If you return late, be prepared to make a fuss at the door," he added. "Charlie locks up at midnight and he sleeps like the dead."

With that smiling admonition he touched his hat at me, and I turned and began threading my way through the crowds.

And such crowds they were—! The sellers of Covent Garden were still in force despite the afternoon hour, describing their fruits and vegetables with barking cries. I could not go ten feet without a sample placed before me. They had competition, however, in the form of the many prostitutes hawking their own wares from the arcades, energetic men arguing in the doorways of coffee shops, and those poor souls who lurched forward from every nook and cranny to ask for aid, some terribly injured. Compared to this muddy chaos, St. Paul's—for I assumed that was the elegant little church at the end of the market—seemed a forlorn beacon of a better world.

I wove my way through the crowd, dancing over droppings and around passersby, nearly colliding with a costermonger loading the last of his day's bruised goods on a cart. He cursed at me and I almost cursed back. Only then did I

realize how very tired I was, and more than a little dizzy. This
morning I had still been on the ship from Newcastle, and
the paltry breakfast we had been served had been my only
food. By the time I was past the church I felt myself visibly
drooping. My exhaustion, at least, left me little with which
to feel anxious.

I had not understood what the coachman meant, only
hoped that it would make sense upon arriving, but he had
not lied. Of the many fine houses lining the street, with their
neatly painted shutters and spotless front steps, only one had
dozens of pamphlets strewn before it. Some had been trampled into the mud, but others were all too clear as to their
content:

The Man Hater's Lamentation
The Adventures of Monsieur Thing

And, perhaps most alarmingly: *On the Heinous Sin of
Self-Pollution*, authored by The Society for the Reformation
of Manners.

A house of unnatural women. I stepped carefully over this
debris and climbed the steps halfway; only then did I see
the tiny, polished plaque that read *Callisto House*—and, I
confess, my nerve nearly failed me then, for only now did it
occur to me that Jo might be here with someone else. What if
she had reunited with a previous lover? I did not doubt that
she would treat me respectfully, but the kindly-worded letter
severing our connection might be halfway to the north, and
here I was on her doorstep.

Yet Jo needed help. What little information I had gleaned

through the day indicated she needed help desperately. I owed her as much, no matter our future.

It was with that resolve that I ascended the remaining stairs and made myself knock firmly, as if I were an invited guest. I barely had time to arrange myself before the door opened halfway, revealing an older woman in the plain garb of a housekeeper. She looked me up and down, then peered out into the street before saying, "Yes?"

"I am here to see Jo Chase," I said, burying my trembling hands under my cloak once again.

She squinted at me again, then stepped aside, just enough that I could push past her. Still, I had to wriggle to fit between the doorframe and her inert form. It was like pressing around a stone column. Once inside, I found myself in a cluttered entryway made smaller by a staircase, its banister covered in a pile of coats and cloaks, pattens in a mound alongside. I could hear the murmur of voices somewhere in the house.

"Name?" She was so close to me I could see the fine grey hairs at her temples.

"Ah, Caroline. Caroline Daniels," I said, wincing at the shudder in my voice, how it only deepened the old woman's squint. Now that I was here, inside, I realized I was trembling not only from nerves but hunger as well, and the airless space was only worsening my tremors.

"Wait here," she ordered, and vanished through a door.

Alone, I gripped the balustrade and dragged my bonnet from my head. Jo was here; she had to be here. I would see her and we would discuss everything calmly, as we always did. Save that Jo was not always calm, and it had been many days now. Lights were flashing in the corners of my eyes, I looked around helplessly for some kind of seat—

Somewhere in the depths of the house was a thump, as of a door hitting the wall, a staccato beat of footsteps, and then the hall door was open and Jo was before me, gaping in astonishment. "Caroline!" she cried. "But how—when—"

I took a step towards her and wobbled. She caught me in her arms and then all was Jo, whispering urgently to tell her what ailed me, calling for someone named Violet as she steered me to the staircase and settled us upon a riser. I was divested of cloak and bonnet and a glass of brandy was pressed to my lips. The drink was warming and wonderful and when I looked at her again her grey eyes were both worried and relieved.

"I am a ninny," I gasped. "Only—"

"Darling, no, never," she interrupted, "I'm the bloody ninny." Before I could retort I was smothered with a kiss that vanquished all my anxieties. When she started to pull away, I flung my arms around her and for a moment we held each other tight, tight, and I could feel her trembling as I was. Oh, that I had ever doubted her, or us!

"But darling, how?" she said into my hair. "I wrote to you, but either the post has wings or—oh God, it's not—is your father—"

"No, no! He was well when I left him." I pressed my hand to her lips, and briefly explained how Mr. Smith's letter had arrived that same day, and both my concern for her and my father's urging had driven me to accept his request. I had thought to leave it at such, but was prodded by her into explaining about the paintings, the murders, the woman and the agent. "But there is nothing more to be done," I finished, "so I am free to help you. Only Jo, what shall we do? They said you might have to sign papers, or, or *flee*—"

A voice cleared behind us, and we turned to see a woman standing in the doorway. "Jo, dear," she said bemusedly, "your food is getting cold."

I jumped, for I had forgotten we were not alone. I jumped, and then found myself blushing before this woman. She was older, yet so elegant as to seem ageless. Her dress was rich, but without any of the ornaments that came and went with the seasons. The opals around her ivory neck seemed nearly to glow, and her carefully arranged hair would have been as appropriate on a girl coming out as on her impressive figure. There was a twinkle of amusement in her eye, but it did nothing to ease my sudden sense of inadequacy.

"Lottie, this is Caroline," Jo said, and I nodded, still blushing furiously.

"I'll have Violet set another place," she declared, and swept back through the door in a froth of silk. I waited until the door closed completely, then laid my hand on Jo's arm.

"I do not wish to impose," I began. "If, ah, your friend—"

"Oh hush," she interrupted. "Lottie can afford to feed another mouth or ten, and if I know Smith he'll have run you all over London without so much as a bun for sustenance. Oh, Caroline." Her voice dropped to a soft whisper. "I am so sorry, darling. That letter so—so *wounded* me, I was so *angry*. All I could think was to get here and shake some sense into Agnes. I told myself it was better that you stay with your father, but in truth I was only thinking of my own hurt, not your feelings or what might come of my leaving. It was unforgivably selfish and thoughtless of me. I'm so sorry."

I nearly said several things, then: phrases like *it's all right* or *of course, I understand*; but it *had* hurt me, and hearing her say so felt like I had been purged of a weight I hadn't known I was carrying. So I merely said, "Thank you for apologizing."

"It's the very least I can do," she replied. Then, more shyly, "Dare I ask how long you can stay?"

"As long as is needed to sort this business with your family," I said, my voice a little sharp, but she was shaking her head.

"I keep hoping, but it seems doubtful it can be sorted," she said. "He is adamant, my sister is desperate to marry him, my mother craves the position he will give her. I am the one obstacle to everyone's happiness, it seems."

"An obstacle to their happiness, and the source of mine," I replied, pleased when she blushed to her roots then. I drew her close, our lips just touching … oh God I was *home*—

"Your food is now cold," a voice reported. We both looked over to see the housekeeper standing in the door, her arms folded.

"My fault, Violet, we're coming," Jo said. She helped me to stand, then kept a steadying hand on my elbow as she guided me through the doorway. Here, a dim parlor led into a brighter dining room, and again I was startled: there was not just Lottie, but a half-dozen people crowded around the dish-laden table, dressed in all manner of costumes. Two in suits, one an elderly woman in full mourning, another in what seemed to be a kind of elegant riding habit, one in a cotton dress even plainer than my own. Atop a buffet was a half-empty soup tureen, a cold leg of meat, and some bowls of salad. Rolls had spilled out of a pretty ceramic basket.

As one, they looked at me and I fought the urge to squirm beneath their scrutiny. From the head of the table Lottie extended her hand to me. "Caroline, darling, I'm so glad you could join us. Please sit down."

"Everyone," Jo announced proudly, "this is Caroline. Darling, these are most of the members of Callisto House. You met Lottie—Lady Audley—and Violet; that is Eliza, Ann, and Bridget; and this is George and Will, they prefer Mister."

At the *Lady* I instinctively curtseyed, inclining my head to hide the flush in my cheeks—how could Jo have been so casual in our initial encounter? George and Will rose and bowed to me, though George did so with an odd stiffness, as if from an old injury. I thought of what Mr. Simmons had told me in Medby, about the women who enlisted as men, who were as men in every sense that mattered. As they settled back in their chairs Jo drew one out for me, then sat beside me. Violet put together a plate of meat and salad, accompanied by a bowl of soup. All was cold, as she had announced, yet delicious nonetheless, and it was all I could do to maintain a veneer of manners as I devoured my meal.

"When did you arrive in London, Caroline?" Lady Audley inquired.

I hurriedly swallowed and said, "Only today. I had, ah, business earlier, then came to find Jo."

"She's looking for a painter, in fact," Jo put in. "A fellow named Loveless."

"Is this more of your spy-work, Jo?" Will raised his eyebrows at us. "Don't tell me you've dragged the poor girl into your business."

"I was not dragged," I said around a mouthful, while Jo replied, "Caroline chooses to come with me, Will, though I suspect it's as much to keep me from swearing as anything."

"Oh, you two are so lovely together!" Bridget, of the plain dress, clasped her hands together. "Jo told us how pretty and brave you are, but she never said you were utterly lovely."

"They're not kittens, Brid," George said, a note of irritation in his voice.

I looked at Jo. "What have you been saying about me?" I asked in a whisper.

"The truth, poorly," she retorted, her voice equally low.

"I never said they were kittens," Bridget said. "Why would you think I was talking about kittens?"

"I have a Loveless," Lady Audley announced. "The one in my boudoir? A portrait of his wife—I believe from when they first met. Ann dear, reach behind you and get me a roll, please?"

The woman in the riding habit twisted in her chair, but before she could reach for the buffet Violet stepped forward and dropped the roll on Lady Audley's plate, then returned to standing in the corner.

"Well. Thank you, Violet," Lady Audley said.

Will leaned towards me. "Don't be fooled, Caroline. Lottie may own this house, but we are here on Violet's sufferance."

"Where did you buy the painting?" Jo asked.

"I bought it from a Mister Gribble, he acts as agent for several painters. He told me quite the story about the wife— Loveless was an old libertine, decades debauched, but soon after they wed his behavior became strange. Started painting places that didn't exist, lost all interest in making sellable work. My painting was one of several she had brought to Mister Gribble without Loveless knowing, just to get enough money to survive. Naturally I had to buy something." She buttered her roll as she spoke. "It's all quite tragic, because I remember seeing Loveless' work before, and it was never as *alive* as what he painted after his marriage. I had thought him mediocre at best, but this one was *remarkable*. I went back to get another, only to find Mister Gribble in a fury. According to him, the wife had cut him out and was selling paintings directly to his clients—paintings, and other goods as well. A tirade which was delivered with many innuendos about my own *fallen* person." She drawled out the *fallen*. "Odious man. But then, what man isn't."

"Her fallen person?" I whispered to Jo, but she shook her head.

My words must have carried, for Lady Audley smiled at me. "Didn't Jo tell you about me, Caroline? Well, suffice to say mine was one of many marriages disrupted by a governess—an old story, save that it was not my husband who instigated the affair but myself. When Stephen found out, we decided to behave in a manner befitting our station and take up separate residences. He kept the manor and I took this house. When he comes to town now he stays at his club."

George mimed dabbing his eyes. "How you have suffered,

Lady Lottie."

"Oh, I have, darling, you cannot imagine." Lady Audley nodded at me. "Finish your food and I'll show you the painting—and I have Mister Gribble's card somewhere as well."

"A thousand per annum's worth of suffering," George said to me.

I became aware of several undercurrents at the table: how Bridget was looking small and ashamed, George's sly tone, Will and Lady Audley's implacable expressions, and the elderly woman—

"Are you all right?" I asked, for there were tears running down her wrinkled face.

At once everyone turned to her, astonished. There were exclamations; Bridget rose from her chair and flung herself around the shaking shoulders; Will poured her a large sherry, while Lady Audley took the small, gnarled hand and stroked it.

"Eliza, darling, is it something we said?" Lady Audley asked gently, but Eliza only shook her head and covered her eyes.

"It's the bickering," Ann said. She had not spoken since I entered the room, had seemed distant and even bored with the company. Her deep voice had a resigned tone to it. "They were always bickering near the end. She hates to hear it now."

"Eliza's … *companion* just passed," Jo said in my ear. "Thirty years together. She had no other family, so Lottie brought her here."

"Oh, the poor creature," I breathed. She seemed impossibly small and frail, the moreso for the others surrounding her. "Can we do anything for her?"

"Other than bring her Margery back?" Jo shook her head. "I don't think so. Come, let's take our drinks upstairs and see this painting Lottie described."

CHAPTER VIII

Portraits

*J*t felt strange to leave the table with Eliza still sniffling, yet Ann had already drifted away and George had procured a small cake from somewhere and was eating it with relish. As Jo and I rose, Lady Audley rose as well, pausing to whisper to Will who was bending over Eliza. We took up glasses of sherry and made our way up the narrow staircase. Here, Jo turned decisively and I felt a small pang. Now that food had restored my wits I could see her easy familiarity with the house. I should have been pleased that she had such a haven, and others who clearly supported her, yet when she strode assuredly into Lady Audley's boudoir I felt a little sick inside.

"It's somewhere—oh." Jo stopped in the middle of the room, staring. I dragged my eyes away from the chaise with its discarded petticoat, the dresser upon which a jewel-laden necklace had been tossed as if as an afterthought—and then I found myself staring as well.

The woman in the portrait looked down at us with a somber expression belying her youth. She was barely a woman, yet Loveless had chosen to paint her with her neckline in disarray and her blond curls loose around her face. But whether her expression was of a lost innocence or merely the painter's instruction, there was no mistaking the pendant around her bare neck: the same design as Thomas Masterson and his conspirators had worn, that Edward Masterson had tattooed on his body.

The stylized face of the monster, Leviathan.

"Bloody hell," Jo swore, and instinctively I grasped her hand, as if together we could deny what was before us.

"We have to tell Mister Smith," I began, but Jo shook her head, glancing behind her as Lady Audley spoke with Violet.

"No," she whispered. "Let's see if Lottie has this Gribble's address and go there first. If we tell Smith," she explained, "he'll just pass it on to Morrow or Windham. If we can bring Loveless to him, or some clear proof that he's involved with these murders? He'll pay us for the additional service."

"But we each have money," I said. "Not a great deal to be sure, but enough if we need—"

To go abroad. But the words stuck in my throat as I thought again of my father.

"I don't." For the first time I saw a hint of tears in her eyes. "Pestell took it all, Caro. He said it would make things easier to put us on allowances. When I argued, he said I hadn't set up the accounts right, we were at risk of losing everything." A tear wound down her cheek. "All my bloody work, and he just swans in! My mother just signed everything he put before her without saying a word ... how could she be so, so *stupid?*"

I hugged her, but before I could speak, Lady Audley said from behind us, "It's the first thing they do, darling, I warned you." She drifted into the room, making her hands into scissors. "Snip the purse strings, and then they can do as they please with you. Your mother is a fool. She was widowed! Every woman's dream! And she gives it all away to fill Pestell's coffers." At my confusion she explained, "He's of age to be sure, but the father rides him over every penny. A wife's income, even a modest one, would give him quite a bit of freedom."

We had nothing to say to that devastating speech, nor did Lady Audley seem to expect us to respond. She kept moving past us to stand before the painting. Now I saw, too, that the tree behind the sitter looked familiar. It was half-obscured by her face, but its graceful branches seemed to echo the oak tree from the other paintings. I looked at Jo and surreptitiously sketched the branch shape in the air. She nodded and mouthed, *Same one, I think.*

"Sometimes I think I bought this because it feels like a mirror," Lady Audley said. "I was so young when I married, so ignorant." She glanced at Jo. "The girl's in trouble, isn't she?"

"Possibly," Jo said carefully.

"Or maybe she reminds me of you …" Thankfully Lady Audley turned back to the painting, for I could not control my outraged expression. Jo's sigh and rolled eyes did little to ease my annoyance. "Do be gentle with her, if you can? Too young! All of us too young." She sniffled audibly.

"How much wine have you had?" Jo demanded. "We just want to talk to this Gribble, Lottie. That's all."

"I have had a quantity befitting my station, thank you very much," Lady Audley retorted. She went to a side table and rummaged through the drawers, finally coming up with a card that she held out—but when Jo went to take it she snatched it back. "Have you decided yet?"

"No," Jo said, sighing again. "And I'm not deciding today, so you can just give me the card."

"She has to leave England," Lady Audley said to me, twisting as Jo swiped for the card again. "I know this type of man, Caroline. They hate anything that threatens their little dominions. Career or no, he will never stand for a tommy in the family. He'll marry her to some controlling brute or he'll put her away."

The words, so bluntly stated, made me flinch. "That cannot be the sum of it," I said, but my voice sounded small. Jo took the opening, however, to grab the card and stick it in her pocket.

"It's not," she said, glaring at Lady Audley. "You can't paint everyone with the same brush, Lottie."

"Perhaps not everyone," Lady Audley replied, returning Jo's gaze.

A silence fell, thick with meaning. I felt suddenly, deeply uncomfortable, an interloper on some private moment. I turned to the door, thinking to leave them alone—

But Jo's hand seized mine and held it tight, keeping me close to her.

"I think we will retire, Lady Audley," she said. "And with thanks for your hospitality, we'll be on our way in the morning."

A flush touched Lady Audley's cheeks, just the slightest hint of darkening. Whatever lay within that silence was severed. She inclined her head and Jo led me from the room. Neither of us looked back.

Jo led me up an even narrower staircase to a small third-story room. Here, a bed was wedged into a corner and her hat and coat hung on a hook by the door. Otherwise, the room was devoid of anything personal, and I hugged her again as I remarked on it.

"Ran from the house with the clothes on my back," she said wryly. "Again, I wasn't thinking." Her arms slid around my waist, drawing me close as she kicked the door closed behind us. "I need my country girl to guide me."

"To tell you to always bring a change of linen," I said, "even when fleeing your brother-in-law."

"*Future* brother-in-law," she growled against my neck, her breath making me giggle. "Agnes hasn't married the sod yet."

Hearing her sister's name reminded me. "Jo," I whispered, "it was Agnes who told me to look for you here."

"Really?" She drew away, frowning. "I didn't know she knew about … this. But if she knows where I am—then she's been giving me time, and she won't want to give much more. The banns have already been printed. They're hoping to marry in a fortnight." She looked around, as if expecting Agnes to appear. "Well, between her and Lottie, there's no returning here."

"You could come to Mister Smith's."

"If he lets me through the door." At my surprise, she shrugged. "Pestell is advancing rapidly, Caro. Smith will want him as a friend, not an enemy. For that matter, so might Lottie."

At the name, pronounced with such familiarity, I blurted out, "Jo. Did you—you and Lady Audley …"

She laughed then, low and soft. "Don't be upset, darling," she said. "Think of Diana Fitzroy, and how close you two were—and how much she helped you understand who you are, even if she was so bad in other ways."

"So Lady Audley was bad for you?" It was all I could do to form a sentence, so deftly were her hands teasing at my laces.

"Lady Audley is a charming, generous woman, who believes she knows what's best for everyone, no matter their own wishes," she explained, tracing the line of my neck with her lips.

"Oh," I said, for something to say.

"She helped me when I first needed to become Jonathan—helped me get papers, helped me find a discreet tailor." We both sighed as my lacings came loose. At once, her hands were underneath, stroking, feeling. "Oh darling," she breathed in my ear. "My beautiful, beautiful Caroline."

"But you didn't want to be with her?" I whispered. For I could not quite believe it—a beautiful, wealthy woman, able to keep her own society—

"Lottie is used to being pleased," Jo murmured. "She likes to dress her lovers, determine where and how they socialize, even dictate their mannerisms." She kissed me. "With you, I can be myself, my best self. There is no comparison."

I opened my mouth to speak—to say something—but Jo had dropped to her knees before me. With a flourish, she undid my petticoats and let them puddle at my feet. As she pushed up the hem of my shift, I closed my eyes and gave myself over to not speaking at all.

CHAPTER IX

Mr. Gribble

*W*e left Callisto House soon after sunrise, stepping out into a chill fog that lay thick in the streets. We had slept little, for reasons first pleasant, then less so as we contemplated the forces arraying against us. It was well before dawn when Jo rose and drew on her jumps, pulling them tight across her chest, and I joined her in dressing. By the time she was dabbing on the ash she used to give herself a hint of sideburns my fancy was turning every creak of the floorboards into Mr. Pestell and his men, and it was with relief that we left the tiny attic room.

As we did so, we nearly stepped upon a note that had been slid under our door. When Jo perused it, her worried expression softened and she held it out to me with a little smile. It was a letter from Lady Audley to Mr. Gribble, asking him to help her dear friend bearing the letter, who was looking for his distant relation Richard Loveless. It was as perfect a ruse as we could ask for, and I felt a touch of shame for my jealousy.

Thus armed, we slipped into the foggy streets. The soft grey air seemed a protection against all scrutiny. In my weary state, I fancied that we could just keep walking and find ourselves in some other land, someplace where a woman could do as she pleased and her family would simply love her. Was there such a place in the world? I had never longed to travel, had been more interested in pirate tales and romances than accounts of expeditions, but finding such a place seemed worth the hardships.

As it was early yet, we found a seller with pasties still warm from the oven and ate our purchases on the steps of St. Paul's while watching the square come to life. In the thin light, people were busily setting up their wares for the day, talking among themselves and calling hails to new arrivals. Too, there were buyers: older women trailed by scullery maids with baskets, a fellow with a small wagon. "Cooks and servants," Jo said by way of explanation. It was so pleasant just to sit and watch. A man emerged from one of the little side doors and with a nod at us began to sweep the portico. Through the half-open door I glimpsed the church's dim, quiet interior and felt immediately drawn to it. I had been attending services with my father, but more from duty than desire. Now I had a sudden urge not only to enter but to pray: out of gratitude for my reunion with Jo, or to ensure my father's continuing survival, or—? I could not say, and I would never know, for Jo touched me on the arm and told me it was time.

The Turk's Head Tavern was not far, about twenty minutes winding away from Callisto House, but it was enough to freshly splatter the skirts I had painstakingly brushed the night before. Hopefully the fact that we were both in sore need of fresh clothing would not undermine our ruse.

At last we reached yet another church, this one with a sign

in both English and Greek—appropriate, as we stood upon Greek Street. Across was the Turk's Head, its sign proudly displaying a dismembered head on a plate. I wondered at such proximity, but when I remarked upon it, Jo simply said, "That's London for you." Whatever the circumstances of the neighborhood, it had not hurt business at the tavern: there was already a man half-asleep outside, stupefied by drink.

As we drew near to the tavern door, however, we saw a familiar figure approaching from the opposite direction and Jo groaned aloud. Mr. Morrow strode forward purposefully, his eyes focused on the ground before him, but when he glanced up and saw us he touched his hat to us, and Jo did the same. He looked much as he had in Medby, though his brown face seemed less weathered, but there was that same slight curling of his lips, as if he were forever bemused at the world.

And perhaps it was that perpetual half-smile that made my stomach knot. He was the only other person, besides Jo, that I had told about killing the man aboard the *Leviathan*, and his response had been so casual that at times I doubted the wisdom of having done so. I had wanted chastisement; instead I had received compassionate indifference.

"Bloody hell," Jo swore. "How did you get here?"

He just smiled that maddening smile and bowed. "Ladies." When Jo put her hand on her hip, he gave a little shrug. "We each have our methods, it seems."

"Is your method named Smith?"

"Actually, it is not," he replied. "Though he did state that if our paths crossed this morning, I was to ask you to see him at your earliest convenience. He wants a word."

Jo exhaled. "And how did he know we would be here?" When Mr. Morrow merely shrugged again she exhaled more violently.

"Now, now," he chided, "surely there's enough work for three? Apparently both victims were stabbed nine times each. Not the kind of fellow I would want to encounter alone."

"I'm surprised you would bother," Jo said, "when you have a warm French featherbed to return to?"

"Not as surprised as I," he replied, then smiled again. "And that reminds me: Madame Viart sends her tenderest regards."

At her name I felt my face heat. To Mr. Morrow I had given my confidences; to Madame Viart I had given something far worse: a promise with no parameters. *An unwritten promissory note, from you to me.* I knew someday she would find a way to call in that promise—at the moment when it most benefitted her.

Mr. Morrow reached for the door, but Jo laid a hand on his arm. "Look, Morrow, I know we work for the same employer, but quite frankly, I need the money—badly. Can't you just bugger off?"

"Escaping to the Continent? That's an expensive proposition."

"As you can personally attest," Jo replied tartly. "So what will it take for you to leave? We can come to some arrangement, I'm sure."

But Mr. Morrow only groaned at her words. "Windham bet me you'd try to bribe me," he said. "Not an hour out of bed and I'm already out of pocket."

"Oh, boo hoo. Some of us have greater problems—"

"—and we are wasting the morning," I said. "Besides, it would behoove Mister Morrow to be on his best behavior; we have a letter of introduction to the gentleman."

His eyebrows raised. "That is an advantage, to be sure. I, however, have been given a different form of introduction." He tapped his coat pocket, making an audible clinking. "One that might get me further than a letter."

"So, what's your story?" Jo asked.

"A merchant who just made a most promising match, looking to furnish an apartment in keeping with my new station. Yours?"

"As if you'll ever settle down," Jo said. "We are distant relations of Mister Loveless, looking to find him."

"Not bad. Want to wager who will find Loveless first?"

Jo pursed her lips. "Perhaps—"

"May I remind you both that men are being murdered," I put in, now irritated. Did this infuriating man bring out the worst in everyone? "The sensible thing to do is to combine our efforts. Together we have both a legitimate reason for asking questions and the money to make it worth his while."

"Sensible, though boring," Mr. Morrow said. "However, I yield to your experience in these matters. Consider me a local friend with a purse, and use me as you see fit."

The last phrase twisted slyly in his mouth, and Jo gave him a smack on the arm before opening the door for me. As she ushered me in I saw Mr. Morrow glance up at the sign, with its bloody, brown-skinned head. For a brief moment the smile vanished and I saw something else, a kind of disgust, and felt ashamed at my own lack of reaction. It was an obscene picture, and how many more did he encounter every day, images I walked past without noticing? I thought to say something—but then we were inside and when I looked at Mr. Morrow he was once again bemused by all before him.

Inside I found a surprisingly clean establishment, in all likelihood due to the young woman vigorously scrubbing a table. The windows had been opened to let in fresh air and there was a strong smell of frying food. A few men were seated separately, each enjoying their breakfasts with half-pints or chocolate, perusing papers or reading books. Only in one corner did we see evidence of what must have been quite a night, in the form of two young men with ink-stained hands and a pretty girl asleep between them. They were trying very hard to drink, but sleep kept pulling their heads down.

Jo spoke to the woman, who pointed at a tiny, portly man whose doughy face was already reddened from ale. His suit was of a crisp wool with embroidery that spoke of continental tastes, his wig was freshly powdered, his cravat spotlessly white even in the dim morning light. He was eating an astonishing number of eggs. When he looked up and saw the three of us, his face took on a practiced expression of polite inquisitiveness.

"Mister Gribble?" At his assent, Jo bowed. "I am Mister Read. This is my wife, and my good friend Mister Morrow. Lady Audley encouraged us to make your acquaintance, with regards to a painting she purchased from you."

"Indeed." He took the letter Jo proffered, his eyes flicking over the contents before he tucked it into his coat. "You are a relation of Richard Loveless?"

"A most distant one, to be sure. But we are recently arrived in London, and thought to call on him. And our good friend Morrow—" She angled her head at Mr. Morrow, who bowed slightly. "—asked to come along, possibly to add to his burgeoning collection."

At the last, a gleam appeared in Mr. Gribble's eye; still he regarded us for a moment before rising. "Then we should probably go to my studio," he said, and with that pronouncement placed a few coins on the table, fitted his hat to his head, and walked out of the tavern, not looking to see if we followed him.

We stepped back out into a busier street where we were immediately accosted by a half-dozen small boys asking Mr. Gribble for errands. He shooed them away with a regal wave and, turning a corner, led us to a nondescript house a few doors down. He ushered us into a vestibule not unlike that of Callisto House, crowded by narrow stairs darkened from years of polish, but quite clean nonetheless. Etchings and paintings were dotted along the stairs, rising into shadow.

"If you please," he said. "My studio and office are at the top."

Jo and Mr. Morrow stood aside, letting me ascend first. As I climbed the stairs my eyes flickered over the images. There were small, intricate copies of what must have been fine landscapes and historical scenes. As we ascended, however, the images became both more sensuous and more crude. There were paintings of couples frolicking in blotchy, yet recognizably pastoral landscapes, and not a few of young women alone in their boudoirs, their clothes in artful states of disarray. At the top of the stairs, Mr. Gribble unlocked a door and ushered us into a surprisingly bright room with comfortable chairs, a broad desk, and several canvases on easels. Here were some of the originals whose etchings hung in the stairwell, and another canvas half-completed, showing a finely rendered woman's face, but with the folds of her clothing merely sketched in.

"I'm not sure to what extent Lady Audley explained my business," Mr. Gribble began. He gestured to a small table upon which a decanter and glasses rested. "Sherry?" When we demurred, he continued, "I am an artist's agent. I have several artists whose works I recommend to my clientele. I also broker portraits, as you see, and in addition to my primary artists I have agreements with specialists—in drapery for instance, or skies. Too, I often step in when a contract is broken, arranging for the completion of half-finished works. My fees in all these matters are quite modest. I pride myself on being able to bring great art into any home or business, no matter my client's station in life.

"But you were asking about Richard Loveless," he continued before any of us could speak. "I was his agent for many years. Indeed, he was the artist who made me realize there was a need for such a person. A good painter, but no ability to make connections, and his tendency to debauchery ensured that once he gained entrance in a household he would soon be ejected. Allowing me to handle his sales brought him a comfortable living."

"But you are no longer his agent?" Jo asked.

"Of course not," Mr. Gribble replied. "Richard Loveless is dead."

"What?" Mr. Morrow blurted out, to which Jo and I both gave him admonishing looks. "We did not know," Jo explained to Mr. Gribble. "There has been little contact between our families for quite some time."

"I expect after the marriage. He lost many friends then. But Richard passed, oh, a little more than a year ago? A boating accident." Mr. Gribble looked at us keenly. "A painful loss, the moreso for having come into his true talent so late in life. He was always a decent painter, but when he finally married—well. I don't know what she did to him, but he came back from France babbling about someplace called Arcadia. He believed it was 'the true England'—pure fantasy—and yet at the same time he began painting with a depth of talent I never knew he possessed."

"We have not met his widow," I said, choosing my words with care.

"Then you are the better for it. I must warn you, if you are thinking to make any claims to his works, you'll have quite a time of it. She's selling his canvases directly, though for the life of me I cannot think how she became acquainted with her buyers. Why, she was here just a few days ago, demanding I give up the painting of Richard's I still have, and when I mentioned I had an appointment with Gerald Vacher, the importer? She went into a fury, saying she, too, was meeting with him, and that I was deliberately interfering." Mr. Gribble shook his head. "Poor Richard," he added.

"Do you know where she lives?" Jo asked.

"I know where they *lived*. I do not know if she still resides there. Before he met her, he was just a few streets away, very convenient. You would often find him drinking with Hogarth and his circle. When they returned from France, however, she insisted they move to the countryside—said the fresh air would soothe his temperament. We hardly saw him after that."

He went to his desk and wrote an address on a slip of paper. As he did so, I said, "I believe it is Missus Loveless' portrait that Lady Audley owns."

"Yes," Mr. Gribble said, waving the paper to dry it. "You can see traces of his old hand in it, but definitely a transitional work. He painted it just before they went abroad."

"Were they in France long?" Mr. Morrow inquired.

"Several months. Whatever transformation she intended to put him through, it seemed to require removing him completely from his milieu." He handed the address to Jo. "It's just north of Tyburn."

"Thank you," Jo said, then, "could we see the one you have?"

"The Loveless? Certainly." Mr. Gribble went to a far corner of the room, where there were several framed canvases leaning against a wall. "I had taken it down in case she returned."

He selected one of the smaller ones and carried it to us. I moved near Jo in instinctive anticipation. And then Mr. Gribble held the painting up to us and I gasped aloud before I could catch myself.

It was the kind of painting one might hang in an alcove, or above a table—hang it, and then do little more than glance at it. But to Jo and I, it was a record of impending violence. It showed a cliffside above churning waters, the rocky front curving to form a bay. Off to one side was a dark smudge that might have been the shadow of an overhang—or an entrance into the cliff face itself.

Though there was no indication of such, I knew—I *knew*—that if one were to scale those cliffs and start walking, turning right would soon bring my own house into view. Turning left would soon reveal the then-whole facade of Harkworth Hall.

Richard Loveless had sat in a boat—close enough that I might have seen him while walking!—and sketched out the whole of the cliff face, showing where the secret tunnel came out, how far it was from the water's surface—

"It is remarkable," Jo said, her voice a little loud. Surreptitiously, she placed a hand on the small of my back, a steadying warmth that calmed me.

"A most subtle work," Mr. Gribble agreed, "far more subtle than anything from before his marriage. The coloring, I think, truly captures the bleakness of the North, as your wife's reaction showed." The hand on my back pressed a little harder at *bleakness*, quelling my retort. "One can only imagine what he might have created had he lived."

"He drowned soon after, then?" Mr. Morrow asked. He, too, was studying the painting, though the significance was lost on him.

"He drowned in that very bay, I'm afraid," Mr. Gribble said, and Jo and I exchanged a look. An early sacrifice? Or silencing a collaborator who knew too much? "You saw the etching on the stairs, of the couple picnicking? A most popular print, based on an early work of his. Perhaps that will help you understand the remarkable development of his talent that his marriage seemed to inspire."

"It is astonishing," Mr. Morrow said with feeling. We all turned to look at him. He was beaming at Mr. Gribble. "Never have I seen such coloration, such depth of feeling— and for such a cold, barren location! It is as if a great well-spring of emotion infused his hand."

I coughed loudly, glaring at him, but he ignored me. Mr. Gribble smiled back, for the first time with real warmth. "That is it, sir. That is it exactly."

"Would you consider selling it?"

"Pardon?" Mr. Gribble blinked at him.

"As Mister Read said, I have my own collection. A humble effort to be sure, but this would be a marvelous addition. A last, great work of a great talent." He continued to smile. "Name your price."

I started to speak—we had the address, what did the painting matter?—but Jo's hand pressed once more.

"I—I am not certain," Mr. Gribble began slowly. "It is the last work I have by him, it may be his last painting ever—"

"Consider, then, that in my collection it would be safe from the schemes of his widow," Mr. Morrow put in. "And certainly many of my friends, both here and abroad, will want to know where I acquired such a skilled work, with an eye towards their own estates?"

At the word *estates* the gleam returned to Mr. Gribble's eye. "May I ask what your business is, sir?"

"Oh, I buy, I sell …" Mr. Morrow waved a hand grandly. "I am known to Vacher, among others. He can vouch for the scope of my dealings."

Still studying Mr. Morrow, Mr. Gribble tucked the canvas under one arm and walked to the desk, where he wrote a number on a piece of paper. He held it out to Mr. Morrow, who merely glanced at it.

"Done," Mr. Morrow said.

Mr. Gribble started, clearly astonished. "Of course you will need time to gather such an amount—"

"No, no, I have it right here." He drew out the wallet from his pocket and began spilling guineas on the desk like a child revealing his hoard. "Perhaps you could draw up a bill of sale while I count these?"

Still looking astonished, Mr. Gribble rested the canvas against the desk, and then with a flick of his coat settled himself to write. Mr. Morrow glanced at us. "If you prefer to wait downstairs—? This will only take a moment."

Jo bowed to Mr. Gribble and led me out to the staircase. It was not until we had descended halfway that she muttered, "Good God, he's been walking around London with a fortune! Smith never entrusted me with that much coin."

"I feel like we missed something," I said. "Did we miss something?"

"He seems to believe there is more to get out of that painting, but I cannot think what." Jo opened the street door and we stepped outside, drawing out the paper Mr. Gribble had given her. "And I have no idea where this is. We'll have to go to Tyburn and start asking directions. God, is this a hanging day? The crowd will be impassable."

I peered over her shoulder, looking at the elegant script.

"Isn't it odd," I murmured, "how everyone refers to Missus Loveless as his wife, or his widow, or the girl? Can no one address her by name?"

"We don't even know her first name, do we?"

"Not even Lady Audley seemed to know."

"Call her Lottie," Jo said. "Keeps her from getting airs."

"I will call her Lady Audley, thank you," I said primly.

Jo grinned at that. She drew close, nuzzling my hair. "Is my country girl jealous?"

"Absolutely not."

"You get this lovely color in your cheeks when you're jealous."

"I am not jealous."

"It is a perfect turnabout for having to watch you with Diana Fitzroy at that dinner party."

I glanced at her then. "You were watching me at the dinner party?"

"Oh, was I ever." Her voice was a purr. "And thinking the most scandalous thoughts—"

A throat cleared and we jumped to find Mr. Morrow still beaming, his hands clasped behind his back like a contented patriarch. "Shall we go?" he asked.

"Where is the painting?" I asked.

"Being delivered to an expert—not that Mister Gribble needs to know such things."

"Right. Do you know the area around Tyburn—" Jo began, but he shook his head.

"As Miss Daniels—pardon me, Missus Read—said, men are being murdered," he said chidingly. "Surely that should be our first concern."

"Which is the point of finding Missus Loveless," I said.

"Ye-es. But I have two letters of my own …" He made a show of feeling his pockets, first producing something with a seal that he held up and studied. "Not that one," he said, carefully putting it back and feeling his coat again, patting his pockets and chest with a studious frown until Jo muttered, "For fuck's sake, Morrow," and I said, "Jo!" Only then did he produce a smaller paper with a flourish, snapping it open and dangling it before us.

"The nine men from the Mastersons' books," he said in an ominous whisper. "I think the name in question is about halfway down—?"

"You think she's going after this Vacher?" Jo asked.

"A few days ago Mister Gribble announced plans to call on him. I would wager that bumped him up the list." He arched an eyebrow at us. "Care to lay odds that we might cross paths with the painter's widow this very day?"

CHAPTER X

Thwarted

"Gerald Vacher." Mr. Morrow held up the paper to the window as our hackney-coach rattled through the streets. "Importer of spirits who believes the tariffs on French wine are a deliberate plot to keep Englishmen pickled in gin. That his father hailed from a family of French vintners has of course no bearing on his views.'" He snorted at the latter.

"And he supported Thomas Masterson's plot?" I asked.

"Five hundred pounds' worth of support," Mr. Morrow confirmed. "Never proved, of course."

"So you think this is all retribution of some kind?" Jo asked. "Justice being meted out to those who escaped charges?"

"That, or …" I trailed off as I realized Mr. Morrow had not seen the portrait in Lady Audley's boudoir, nor did he understand the significance of the bay painting. If Loveless had been intimate with the Mastersons, he may have shared their fantastic beliefs—and infected his wife as well.

"I think," Mr. Morrow said carefully, "it is a little early to ascribe motive."

Jo frowned. "You know something that you're not telling us."

"And you know something you're not telling me," he replied.

"Come now—"

"I'm no dull-swift, Chase," he said, then pointed at me. "And don't ever let that one near a gaming table, unless you want to lose your shirt."

"I hardly think that's a concern," I snapped. Though perhaps I was being rash. A year ago I would have sworn that I would never set foot in a brothel … or murder anyone.

Jo and Mr. Morrow were staring at each other, with equally narrowed eyes. Slowly, as if she were in a crosshairs, Jo leaned over to me. "Do we tell him?" she whispered.

"Not yet," I whispered back, loud enough for him to hear. "Let him stew a while longer."

My words earned me a decidedly rude gesture, and I was further irritated to find myself burying my hands in my cloak lest I respond in kind. Too long with him and I would be as uncouth as a soldier, and how much worse would Jo become?

But we were saved from further demonstrations of Mr. Morrow's wit by the coach halting. We found ourselves outside an older house, timbered and sprawling. I could hear the river close by. "How convenient," Jo said, "he can bring his wine right to his doorstep."

"It has certainly been a motley assortment of conspirators," I said as she disembarked, then helped me out.

"There are an astonishing number of professions who gain from warmongering," Mr. Morrow said as he leapt out behind us. "I doubt they had to go far to find willing investors."

At the door, I knocked while Jo looked around warily. "It seems unusually quiet," she said. "Wasn't Smith supposed to be alerting the remaining men?"

Mr. Morrow's reply was cut off by the door opening, revealing a young man in his shirtsleeves, a pen still clutched in one hand. "Look," he said as he opened the door, "I already told you—oh. Now what?"

"We would like to speak to Mister Vacher," I said.

"You and everyone else this morning! He's not available." He started to close the door but Jo stuck her foot out.

"It's important," she said. "Trust me, it's very much to his advantage."

"That's what the other fellow said, and trust *me*, if he wouldn't see a messenger from the government, he certainly won't see you." He began pushing on the door, and Jo casually leaned her shoulder on it.

"I think he'll appreciate hearing what we have to say," she said.

This time he squinted at her, and then a sly smile broke over his face. He looked up at Mr. Morrow. "Did old Watley put you up to this?" he asked. "Not that he's adverse to daytime play, but he's already being entertained, by prettier goods than what you're offering."

"I beg your pardon—" I began, horrified, but Mr. Morrow held up a hand.

"You can let us in," he said calmly, "or I can go back to the magistrate and get some constables and a writ, and you can tell us all about Watley and his goods in Newgate. Your choice."

The man scowled. "You black—"

But his epithet was cut off by a decidedly female shriek of—terror? Fury? It sounded like both at once, and more. It made all of us shudder, and to a one we looked to the stairs leading from the hall.

With a cry Jo shoved as hard as she could, bending over so Mr. Morrow could throw his fist at the young man. He fell backwards clutching his nose and the three of us tumbled inside. Jo was up the stairs first, Mr. Morrow on her heels producing from somewhere on his person a small pistol. On the landing they halted, unsure of which door to attack, until we heard a hoarse moan, this time in a male voice. Mr. Morrow pushed ahead, holding up the pistol with a raised eyebrow when Jo started to protest. She shook out her sleeve and a knife appeared in her hand. I cleared my throat and showed Mr. Windham's blade. He grinned at us both, but took the lead nonetheless.

We crept towards the door at the end of a little hall. As we neared it, the young man appeared behind us. "You can't go in there," he said. He had a vast, bloody handkerchief pressed to his nose. "He's entertaining."

"He's being murdered," Mr. Morrow snapped. "For God's sake, man. Is this the room?"

Startled, the man nodded. Mr. Morrow threw himself forward, knocking the door in and skidding into the room, Jo and I close behind.

The first thing my eyes alighted on was a plump, middle-aged man, his breeches unbuttoned and his shirt soaked in blood, twitching on the floor while the crimson pool expanded beneath him—

—and it was the *Leviathan* all over again: I could feel his blood on my hands, I could feel the life slipping from his body, that shuddering that was as much terror as the frantic beating of his failing heart—

"Caroline." Jo stepped before me, her hands resting on my arms. "Caro, look at me."

I blinked. I could not stop staring at the man, but she touched my face and forced my gaze away. Her grey eyes warm, her hand warm. "Caro, there's nothing you can do," she said softly. "Take a breath, love. That's it," she cooed as I inhaled with a shudder. "That's my country girl. Now let it out, and take another."

As I breathed again, smoother this time, she gave my arms a squeeze. "You cannot save him," she whispered. "And that is not your fault. He is not your fault. Let him go to his Maker now, and let's try and stop this ugly business before anyone else gets killed."

I had not stopped taking deep breaths. At the last I nodded, though I did not feel so resolved. When I looked again at the floor I saw that the body had been covered by a blanket, and Mr. Morrow was trying to get a description of the woman who had delivered the painting that morning; I heard *blonde* and saw the man sketch curves in the air. Jo snorted. "Well, so much for useful information. Now where's that bloody painting—oh, damn!"

The painting had been propped near the fireplace. In the struggle it must have been knocked askew—for it was a struggle, I saw: there were smeared footprints, large and small, peeking out from beneath the blanket. The heat of the fire had set the canvas smoldering, the paint blossoming into dark, smoky clouds. The same tree on a hill with the sea in the distance, the same somber boys and their father, but the mother was gone, and a yellow and white smudge was *moving down the hill*—

The figure looked back at us, she *saw* us, and God help me all I could think was, *she's terrified*—

Jo gasped and instinctively reached for the spot but I snatched her hand back before she could be burned. The smudge vanished in a bloom of fire, but we had both seen it. We looked at each other and nodded in confirmation.

"Yellow," Jo whispered. "I saw yellow, and a face."

"Blonde," I whispered, touching my head. I looked once more at the blackening canvas, and the brass plaque at the bottom of the frame: *In Arcadia*.

We turned to see Mr. Morrow crouched by the corpse, holding up a corner of the blanket to peer beneath. "I can hear you two whispering," he said, not raising his eyes. "Have I stewed enough?"

"You have," Jo said. "We need to get to the Loveless house."

Mr. Morrow instructed the young man, who turned out to be Mr. Vacher's secretary, to send for Mr. Smith, and left a note for him. Then we hurried to the nearest avenue to find another hackney coach. Only when we had gotten inside, and Mr. Morrow had negotiated with the driver and bade him to make haste, did he fold his arms and fix us both with his glare. "Out with it," he said.

"Only if you tell us what you know," Jo replied.

He hesitated, sucking his teeth. The coach bounced over a rough stretch of road and we all tumbled about. When we righted ourselves, he said, "I don't know anything, as such. My sister is an artist—she draws and paints subjects for etchings. She remembered seeing Loveless' work when she was taking lessons, and she did not think this sounded like him—he was decidedly more, ah, *licentious* in his projects, and openly disdainful of portraiture." He hesitated again. "I also have a theory, but I'll know that answer by suppertime."

Jo nodded. "Fair enough. The Loveless widow, at least, was somehow part of the Masterson cult. We saw her portrait. She wore a pendant of that symbol of theirs. And that bay is near Caroline's house, where Edward Masterson kept the beast."

"Not necessarily a willing part," I put in, thinking of that young, terrified face.

Mr. Morrow nodded. "Well. That makes it much more tidy."

"And we too have another theory—" Jo looked at me for confirmation and I nodded, thinking of how the paintings moved. "—but perhaps we will save that as well for the evening revelations? Our concern now is finding the widow."

"Agreed." He fixed us both with his gaze. "If we do find her, we are duty-bound to bring her to Smith. Are we agreed on that as well?"

"Without harming her," I said.

"Miss Daniels, she may have murdered three men—"

"Or she may merely be the vehicle for another's ill intent," I interrupted. "Without harming her, Mister Morrow." There was an edge to my voice now.

He looked at Jo, but she only spread her hands. He sighed and nodded once. "If possible," he said, and there was enough finality in his voice, and reason behind his words, that I said no more.

CHAPTER XI

Answers

*O*ur hackney coach would only take us as far as Tyburn gate. Here we disembarked and, after some consultation with the gatekeeper, proceeded further down the road. In doing so we arrived at the terrible Tyburn tree, such a staple of song and broadside that even we in the distant North knew of it. There were still bits of rope clinging to its frame, and the dirt around it was freshly trampled. Jo said, "Did we miss one yesterday, then?" and Mr. Morrow said, "No, it was the day before," and I wondered at their casual apprehension of such a terrible place. The footprints in the dirt suggested a crowd of hundreds. There were towering wooden stands stained and muddied from wear, forming an outdoor theater. The inn at the corner offered special hanging day prices for food, drink, and lodging.

"My father took me to my first hanging at seven," Mr. Morrow said, as if reminiscing about a holiday.

"I was ten, and I had to sneak over myself," Jo said with a chuckle.

"You are both callous," I put in. "Why would you ever want to witness such a thing?"

"My father believes that it is every subject's duty to stand witness," Mr. Morrow explained.

"I had no such pretensions. It's always a great party. Plenty of food and drink, singalongs and banter …" Jo laughed at my exasperation. "You shall just have to judge for yourself one day."

Our conversation was made more absurd by the fact that we had turned a corner and in doing so had seemingly left London behind us. The road had transformed into a charming country lane, though if I looked behind me I could still glimpse the gallows. The houses were stone cottages, with well-tended fields between them. We could have been in my own little corner of England. Too, I could hear water nearby, a brook or a river, though I could not glimpse it amidst the fields and orchards. It was as sweet a setting as I could imagine.

We came to what appeared to be a village, and a quick word with the publican took us down a narrow footpath. Here, shaded by an oak tree, we found a cottage framed by a crumbling stone wall. Before it was an overgrown patch that had once clearly served as a garden, and the shutters were in need of repair, but the overall building looked sound. Wild roses bloomed from a bramble-filled corner, and the brook burbled happily from behind the house. It was a pretty sight, reminding me of the fairy stories of my youth. If Mrs. Loveless had married unwillingly, she had at least secured pleasant accommodations.

"No one's been here for weeks." Mr. Morrow pointed to the threshold, which was fuzzed with moss.

"She may be using another door, or even a window," Jo

offered. "To give the impression that the property is vacant."

He nodded slowly. "Perhaps using the same technique the murderer is using," he mused.

I glanced at Jo, thinking of the figure in the painting, but she was already moving around the cottage, inspecting the window ledges and peering at the ground. I followed her as Mr. Morrow went the other way, studying the far side of the building. Now I could see mold spattering the window-glass, and inside the ghostly shapes of sheet-covered furniture. Cobwebs laced the window frame.

We were no worse off than we had been at Mr. Vacher's house, yet I felt keenly frustrated, and worried. Though I had barely glimpsed her face, I had the unshakeable impression that the woman who had looked back at us—be she Mrs. Loveless or another—was utterly terrified. But was it the terror of a murderer being pursued, or of an unwilling accomplice to such? Three men dead. I could not imagine the fragile girl of Lady Audley's portrait doing such a thing, but ever since my father brought Edward Masterson into our lives I have learned just how limited my imagination was.

Around the back we found a door even more scummy with moss than the front, for here the oak tree kept all in shadow. A moment later Mr. Morrow appeared, and he shook his head at our inquisitive looks.

"Do we force it, then?" Jo asked. "We should search it, having come all this way."

"Easier to break a window," Mr. Morrow said.

"Easier still to look for a key first, or a window left un-latched?" I offered with a hint of exasperation. "Before we start damaging property?"

He squinted at me, but helped Jo and I search around the door, checking divots in the stonework and feeling under stones and ledges. We plodded back to the front, and so lost was I in studying the windows for a loose casement that I walked right into Jo's back. She had halted in the grass with a hiss of anger that had me grasping my knife before I could think.

Two large, ornate carriages had drawn up at the end of the footpath, one with a coat of arms on its door that I did not recognize but Jo clearly did. She muttered "*shit*" beneath her breath and I seized her hand in mine, alarmed to find it trembling.

Slowly we made our way forward. The carriage doors opened and people emerged: first a pale young man in an elegant suit and hat clutching a gold-topped cane who helped out two women. At the second one my heart sank, for it was Agnes Chase.

And if here was Jo's sister, then the other woman was—her mother? I could see a little resemblance beneath the broad bonnet, but everything about her seemed tight and sharp, unlike Agnes' softness or Jo's lithe movements.

Mr. Morrow stepped close to us. "What the hell is this?" he asked in a low voice.

But neither Jo nor I answered him, for at that moment Lady Audley disembarked from the second carriage and we both winced at this blow. She gave us an apologetic shrug, but otherwise stayed close to the vehicle.

"Well?" Jo's mother strode down the footpath, followed

by Agnes and the young man, her expression grim. "What do you have to say for yourself?"

"Good afternoon, Mama," Jo said, bowing. The gesture only made her mother's expression further darken.

"You will curtsey to your mother," she began, only to wave her hand when Jo started to do just that. "No! Not with your legs—your legs—" Her face reddened alarmingly.

"Mama," Agnes began, but silenced as her mother raised her hand.

"I cannot believe it," her mother went on, spitting the words out. "Staying at that, that *house*, gallivanting around in public dressed like, *like* …" She inhaled deeply, as if struggling to breathe. "We have been looking for you all morning, and what trail have we had to follow? Fallen women and—and *artists* …"

She waved her hand, a loop that encompassed Jo, myself, Mr. Morrow, and the weedy garden, and then sagged as if overcome. Agnes caught her arm to steady her.

"Oh, it's not quite as bad as all that," the young man said. He smiled at Jo, and though his expression was kindly enough my hackles rose. "I haven't seen you since that first dinner. I feel as if we got off on the wrong foot. Can we start again?"

Jo's hand tightened in mine. "It depends on your intent, sir."

"Joanna." He said the name caressingly. "I do understand all this, I really do. My own sister was a bit of a boy growing up—she rode as well as me, loved to hunt, was brilliant at cards." Mrs. Chase moaned audibly at his description. "And now she is a brilliant wife and mother, and her husband is a distinguished Member of Parliament. I'd like you to meet her. I think you two would have a lot in common. And, honestly, she'd be a better source of guidance than—well." He glanced significantly in Lady Audley's direction.

Surreptitiously I looked around us. There was no easy egress from the garden. Between the drivers and the footmen there were four Mr. Pestell could call upon. Mr. Morrow caught my eye: *what the hell* he mouthed again, and I could only shake my head helplessly, trying to blink back my rising tears.

"Joanna, you must come home," Mrs. Chase burst out. "You must come home at once and give this up!"

"Jo, please," Agnes said, and I felt Jo's sharp inhale, as if she had been struck. I understood then that she was the root of it all; she was what kept Jo hesitating, rather than fleeing or appealing to Mr. Smith for help. "Just to try, just for a little while. You used to tell me to try everything once, right? Even disgusting things, like those jellied fish."

At her words Mr. Pestell beamed at her. So there was love there, of a kind.

"And if she doesn't like it?" I asked. "If she's unhappy and wants to leave? What then?"

"Who is this person?" Mrs. Chase demanded.

"This is Caroline, Mama," Jo said, "and I wish to hell I was introducing you under better circumstances."

"We're her family," Agnes was saying. "Why would she be unhappy with us? We love her!"

"I know you've all had a difficult time of it," Mr. Pestell continued, "and things have been asked of you that should never have been asked, Joanna. But I'm here now, and your sister needs *you*—not the brother she never had, but the sister she does." He held out a hand. "Come along now. Whatever you've become involved in, I can make it go away, never fear."

"Or else—?" Jo spread her free hand. "You've taken my money, you made it clear that you would restrict my movements. So what will you do if I don't come?"

"Really, I don't see—" he began.

"Joanna Chase, you stop this nonsense—" her mother began at the same time.

"That's enough," Mr. Morrow barked, making everyone jump. He shoved past Jo and I and snapped out a piece of paper from his coat. "By order of the Crown, I must ask you to stop interfering with His sworn agents in their lawful work." He handed the paper to Mr. Pestell and folded his arms. I had forgotten just how much of a presence Mr. Morrow could be when he chose. It was not for nothing that Thomas Masterson had hired him as his second.

Mr. Pestell read the paper through twice, his expression incredulous. "This is preposterous," he said at last. He looked up at Mr. Morrow, nearly a hand's breadth taller. "I take it you are the Francis Morrow named here?"

Mr. Morrow inclined his head.

"What is it?" Mrs. Chase reached for him, though Agnes tried to hush her. "What does it mean?"

"It means I told you the truth," Lady Audley put in. We all jumped again, having nearly forgotten her. "And I would like to go home now."

"But that's impossible!" Mrs. Chase looked from the paper to us and back, her expression aghast. "The king would never employ women, or …" She looked again at Mr. Morrow, as if not quite sure what he was.

Agnes said nothing, but her face was pale. Jo gave a little shrug. "I did tell you, Aggie," she said. "You can't just pretend a thing away."

"Well. I will certainly be calling on this Smith fellow—" Mr. Pestell broke off as Mr. Morrow promptly held out a calling card, then gestured for the paper to be returned. "Yes. Well."

"I believe he has some time tomorrow afternoon," Mr. Morrow said briskly, shoving the paper back in his pocket. "I will tell him to expect you. Chase, Daniels, we have an appointment to keep."

Without further ado he walked down the path, pushing past Mrs. Chase who gave a squeak of fright. I raised my chin and followed, keeping hold of Jo's hand until I was certain she was right behind me. As we passed them I inclined my head to Mrs. Chase and Agnes, and curtseyed slightly to Mr. Pestell. Behind me, however, Jo paused, and I slowed my steps, sensing Mr. Morrow do the same.

"What did you think would happen, when you asked me to be Jonathan?" Jo's voice was soft, but it carried. "Did you really think that once off the leash, I would ever submit to it again?"

"You were only supposed to be him on *paper*," Mrs. Chase retorted, her voice anguished. "You were only supposed to be a *signature*."

Jo looked at her for a moment, then started walking

again. I felt the knot in my stomach loosen, though I knew the matter was far from settled.

At we passed the second carriage Lady Audley stuck her head out the window. "Sorry, darling," she said, "but he threatened without threatening, if you take my meaning. I have to protect the many before the few."

Jo snorted. "Fuck off, Charlotte," she said, and quickened her pace until she was at my side once more.

Our "appointment" turned out to be a stop at the public house, where we ordered onion soup and toast. Jo and Mr. Morrow had beer and I had a sherry while we waited for our food, sitting silent in a corner until we saw the carriages finally pass. Beneath the table Jo had taken my hand again, though her expression revealed nothing. I desperately wished we were alone so we could talk it all through, try and think of something—

Mr. Morrow had leaned close to the window, watching the carriages depart. Now he sat upright once more and fixed Jo with his gaze. "Chase, I understand not wanting to be beholden to him," he said quietly. "But from what I gather is happening? Smith is the lesser of two evils. If I were you I would get that smug ass off my back, and worry about Smith later." He smiled, but there was no amusement in his eyes. "Remember you have as much on him as he has on you." Jo opened her mouth but he held up a hand. "Just my opinion. I'll say no more."

As much on him. I frowned, trying to think on what he could mean—

—and then I remembered the way Mr. Smith and the other man had looked at each other, and I began to understand. Jo was silent, but her head was bobbing slightly, as if nodding at Mr. Morrow's words, and I suspected that she was coming to a decision—though at what cost, I shuddered to think on.

Our soup and bread appeared, and despite my apprehensions my stomach reminded me that our pasties had been long ago. Even Jo managed to eat, though her somber expression never wavered.

Mr. Morrow downed the last of his beer with relish and ordered a second. "Well. I think a daylight break-in is no longer advisable, that lot will have advertised our presence to the entire village." He smiled at us, and for once it was warm, not his usual sly amusement. "I vote we let Smith search the house, and in the meantime continue on. Since I've had the pleasure of your relations, Chase, may I now offer to inflict my own upon you both?"

CHAPTER XII

And More Answers

We arrived in front of a grocer's, the windows bright with lamplight as the sun began to set. *My father's a grocer in Cheapside*, he had told me in Medby. Through the glass we could see a man and a woman helping customers, both as dark-skinned as Mr. Morrow himself, and the man so close in resemblance as to be a copy. I looked from him to his father and back, but Mr. Morrow ignored my scrutiny, instead cursing as he dug in his pockets for the fare.

"Good Lord, Morrow, you're the spit of him," Jo observed.

"Oh, well spotted, Chase," Mr. Morrow retorted. "Would either of you master spies have twopence?"

I indeed had twopence; we disembarked and waited for Mr. Morrow as he paid the driver. Both of us were silent—I could not speak for Jo, but I felt as if we were somehow intruding. The scene before us, the smiles on the faces of the customers and the Morrows alike, seemed at odds with the Mr. Morrow we knew, who had plotted against Thomas Masterson while in his employ, then worked as a spy in the company of a French bawd.

I thought again of my own father, and silently prayed for his continued health.

Mr. Morrow glanced at the window, but made no effort to greet his parents. Instead he led us down an alley to a yard in the back. Here were stacked crates and barrels in two neat rows with their branded contents clearly visible. Wedged between was a small, snug shed with a light burning inside. Mr. Morrow knocked, then waited, until a female voice cried, "enter!"

He opened the narrow wooden door and ushered us inside—though *inside* was a generous term for the space we found ourselves in, cluttered as it was with an easel, a side table, a stool, two shelves of pigments and brushes, and barely room for us.

Despite all this, the little space was brightly lit by both lamps and daylight from a window fitted in the roof above. The glow illuminated the face of the young woman who greeted us and the complex drawing of twined flowers and vines on the easel behind her.

"Frannie!" She hopped off the stool and hugged Mr. Morrow, her exuberance shoving us against the walls of the little shed and making the whole structure wobble.

Jo took advantage of being crushed against me to kiss me beneath my ear and whisper, "Back to Smith's, after—?" I nodded, kissing her back before Mr. Morrow cleared his throat.

"Helena, this is Misses Chase and Daniels. They're working on this with me."

At *Misses* she looked at Jo curiously, but inclined her head to each of us. Side by side, I could see the striking resemblance between Helena Morrow and her brother: her skin was darker, but they shared the same large brown eyes and delicate mouths, though on Miss Morrow her brother's sardonic smile was softened into merriment. Her black hair was braided charmingly about her face; it made her look elegant despite her paint- and ink-spattered smock. I felt rumpled and dowdy in comparison.

"So?" Mr. Morrow looked around the shed. "Did you get it?"

"Oh, I received it." She gestured behind herself, where the painting from Mr. Gribble's studio leaned against the wall. "What do I get for telling you?"

"Hel, this isn't a game."

"No, it is not!" She smacked his arm. "First, you're in the north, then you're in France, then you suddenly turn up, asking about Richard Loveless, of all people? You cannot just expect us to do for you, Francis Morrow. You have to give as well. So what do I get for telling you?"

He exhaled, looking at us. Jo grinned at him. "The lady has a point, *Frannie.*"

"What do you want," he ground out.

"You can stay the night for a start. Mother has been worried sick about you, the men talk of nothing but war with France." She paused, tapping her lip. "And … you come with us to dinner at Gerald's house."

"Dinner?" He stared at her, incredulous.

"Dinner." She pronounced it with finality. "You haven't done more than wave at Gerald since you went north with that horrible man. But we are going to be family now, whether you like it or not."

"You're engaged, then?" I inquired.

"I've wanted to marry Gerald since we were children," she declared. "And I always get my way."

"The poor bastard," Mr. Morrow muttered, only to get smacked again. "Fine. Tonight, and dinner. Well?"

Miss Morrow held the canvas up to the light. "This," she announced, "is not the work of Richard Loveless."

"Ah," Jo and I said in unison.

"It is certainly his *signature*, but anyone can copy a signature—can't they, Frannie?" She smiled sweetly at him.

He exhaled again, but only said, "So who is the artist?"

"Oh, Penelope, I should imagine." At our confusion she explained, "Richard Loveless' wife. Penelope Brocas, as was. Someone found her in the street doing caricatures for a penny, like some kind of English Giotto, and paid for her to study in France. It certainly has a French feeling, the way the light is handled."

"A woman," Mr. Morrow said wonderingly. I snorted at that, and was pleased when he looked embarrassed.

"Oh, really, Frannie! And what does that make me? Mother runs the store more than Father, and I daresay our aunt's seen more blood than half your soldier friends. She's a midwife," she added for Jo's and my benefit. "Say 'woman' in that tone around her and she'll box your ears."

"If it is her work, that means Penelope has been painting for years under her husband's name," Jo said thoughtfully. "Miss Morrow, have you ever seen a painting appear to move? Is there some technique that could produce such an illusion?"

Mr. Morrow looked at us in surprise, but Miss Morrow

merely frowned, thinking. "You could embed something in the paint—glass, say, or pieces of mirror—that would catch the light. And certainly a well-done portrait can seem like it's looking at you. But otherwise, I cannot think of anything."

We looked at each other and nodded. It had been a last chance at some kind of reasonable explanation for what we had both seen, but the true answer, I knew, lay with Penelope.

Penelope. It felt significant, somehow, to finally have her name.

"Thank you for your help," I said, inclining my head.

"But of course. Unless you want to stay to supper—?" Miss Morrow smiled, ignoring yet another of her brother's exasperated sighs.

"Unfortunately, I have to speak to our employer—as your brother rightfully advised me to do," Jo said ruefully. "Morrow, what do you want to do with the painting?"

"Bring it back with you," Mr. Morrow said. "That way he'll know I wasn't making free with his money."

Jo took the painting, and I took Jo's arm. "Come on," I said, smiling at her grim expression. "Let's go talk to Mister Smith."

It was dark when we finally trudged up the steps of the house in St. James' Square and rang the bell. Charlie let us in, smiling warmly at the sight of Jo beside me and taking the painting before returning for our coat, cloak, and hats. Mr. Windham appeared and waved us into the dining room.

There, Mr. Smith was presiding over an array of half-empty dishes, and rose and bowed when we entered. Mr. Windham started to pull out a chair for me but Jo hesitated in the doorway, and I stayed by her side.

"Sir," Jo said, bowing slightly. "I'm afraid I need your help." There was a hint of a tremor in her voice, but her head was held high.

Mr. Smith nodded. "I suspected as much," he said. "Join us, and eat something." There was no expression on his face save for a slight twitch at the corner of his mouth—a smile? "Everything turns out better when decided on a full stomach."

Jo took my hand and led me to my chair, settling me before sitting beside me. We ate slowly, answering Mr. Smith's questions about Penelope, the painting we had brought, and Miss Morrow's assessment. I could not quite articulate what I believed about the paintings, and Jo had been quiet on our way back—pondering, I surmised, how she would present her situation to Mr. Smith—so I had not broached the topic with her. Thus I said nothing about how the paintings moved, or how the one at the Burton house had felt not only soft but *permeable*, and Jo did not raise the topic either.

"We'll have to start a search for her," Mr. Smith said, looking at Mr. Windham. "It might pay to go to the docks tonight and put out word, in case she decides to make a run for the coast."

"I'll go now," Mr. Windham said, rising. "If you'll excuse me," he added with a bow.

"If you find her, take care," I said. "We don't know if another directs her."

"That may be, but she may also be a murderer," Mr. Smith said. "So yes, take care, both with her and any accomplices she might have."

"I just think—" I began.

"Miss Daniels, I have seen women behave as brutally as men, perhaps moreso. Certainly you know by now what a woman is capable of."

At the last my retort died on my lips, replaced only by a sudden numbness. Did he know? How could he know? Beneath the table, Jo took my hand and said, "Just because a person knows how to use a knife doesn't make them a murderer." She looked at Mr. Windham. "Penelope is young, and this plot—the paintings, the deliveries, the nine blows—it's not impossible that it's all her doing, but it's just as likely she's acting at another's behest. That's all."

Her hand was comforting, and Mr. Windham's nod, seemingly full of understanding, further eased my worries. I could not say why I felt such concern for Penelope, only that I did, and Jo was always saying that my instincts were better than hers.

When we finished eating, Mr. Smith laid his hands on the table. "Well," he said. "I think you and I, Chase, should discuss your situation."

"We can all discuss my situation—" Jo began, but he shook his head.

"Humor me in this," he said. "I would speak to you alone, please. You can tell Miss Daniels anything you like after, but I prefer that this first discussion be between us."

Jo looked at me. I nodded heavily, though my stomach

was twisting. To be barred from their conversation seemed a
return to the circumstances that had first sent her running,
yet what else could I do? We needed Mr. Smith's help and
these were his terms. But as if she could hear my thoughts,
Jo leaned in and whispered, "I will decide nothing without
you, I swear it," and I believed her.

I took a book from Mr. Smith's still-chaotic study and
went to find a place to read before bedtime. Across the hall
was a parlor, and I thought to read there, but at the doorway
I paused. Leaning against a wall were the two canvases from
the murder scenes, now with Mr. Morrow's purchase beside
them.

Putting the book aside, I lit a lamp and brought it close,
studying the images. The two paintings were similar, but
not identical. The woman was missing in both; the rose in
the man's lapel was wilted. In the background of one, the
sea was placid, and there was a shadow halfway down the
hill—a person? While in the second, there were no other
people, but there were strange, lumpish rocks just visible in
the churning surf.

Where was this tree, and this hill? *ARCADIA*, the frames
read. *The true England.* Yet the details were so precise, the
tree branches so similar, that I could not but believe it was a
real place, one Penelope knew intimately.

I began exploring the surface of the first canvas, searching
for any kind of movement, any softness. My eyes darted to

every glistening stroke of paint, every slight shadow, though each seemed to be a product of the texture itself, and the surface stayed rigid beneath my touch …

"Oh, hullo," a man said behind me. I whirled about to find Mr. Smith's friend leaning against the door. "I don't think we've been properly introduced. I'm Oliver."

"Caroline Daniels," I said, my voice catching a little. "I did not hear you enter, Mister, ah—"

"Really, Oliver is fine." He bowed to me, then caught up my hand and kissed it with a flourish. "I suppose you didn't come to tell Jeremy that you have the murderer bound and trussed and ready for trial?" At my confused expression he said, "Your Mister Smith."

"Oh! Yes, of course." *You have as much on him as he has on you.* "I mean, no, no such results yet, but I believe we made progress."

"Well, that's something at least." He cocked his head, studying the paintings, which gave me a moment to study him. His suit was quite stylish, more befitting a young man than one with greying temples peeking beneath his wig. Beneath the powder, his pallid face was starting to show the lines of age. "Stephen Masterson," he said thoughtfully. "Really, you never would have expected his boys to amount to anything, much less the plots Jeremy described."

"You knew him?" I asked, startled.

"Oh yes. Member of Parliament from some rural county or other, terribly arrogant despite it, but then one day he simply vanished. The boys were sent up to school but didn't have the easiest time of it." He shrugged, and I recognized the gesture: it was the easy shrug of a nobleman born, dismissing others' circumstances. Even at our own small assemblies at home I had seen it in the local gentry.

"What about a Penelope Brocas?" I asked. "Have you heard of her?"

"Brocas?" He tapped his chin thoughtfully. "I feel like I've heard that name somewhere, though not a *Penelope* Brocas. Perhaps a relation of the mother? She was from money. Educated in France, Jeremy had Francis Morrow looking into her. That sort of stabbing—it just feels French, wouldn't you say?"

Again the easy shrug. I wasn't sure if he was teasing me, so I merely smiled. "It feels like desperation," I said, and realized it was true as I said it. It was measured, certainly; it was plotted, but there was also something frantic to it all, a feeling of being driven to a breaking point …

"Again, very French," he replied. "And with that, Caroline—may I call you Caroline? Jeremy prefers formality but it's terribly boring—I must away to bed, for I have been dining and drinking and gossiping for hours, and if I don't sleep I shall forget it all and Jeremy will be quite cross with me."

"Well, we wouldn't want that." Despite myself I found myself liking Oliver. Though he had the dismissive ease of someone who has never known worry, there was no malice in it. He seemed quite content being Mr. Smith's eyes and ears, no doubt gathering all sorts of useful information. "I should probably retire as well. It's been a most tiring day."

"Shall we, then?" He crooked an elbow at me. "I will merely walk you to your door. We wouldn't want to make your Jo jealous."

I rolled my eyes, but slipped my arm into his, and we made a companionable ascent to the bedrooms above while I answered his light questions about my village, my family, and whatever did we do for fun in the north? It was not until I had shut the door on him that I realized I had added to his storehouse of information, and even then I could not find it in me to be annoyed. He was just so terribly charming.

CHAPTER XIII

The Empty House

I awoke to Jo's gentle, "Caroline," and her hand rubbing my back. Not my usual awakening by Joanna Chase, which entailed much opening of curtains and striding around the bedroom while she rattled off the day's possibilities. She looked tired and drawn. I glanced at the bed and realized she had not slept.

"There was a lot to talk about," she said in answer to my worried expression. "He wanted to make sure I understood every aspect of my choices, in detail. As if I hadn't thought it all through already."

"And?" I asked.

"And this afternoon I will offer to break off all contact with my family, in exchange for remaining, legally, Joanna Chase." She smiled sadly. "It's the only way forward, I think. If I keep using Jonathan there's always a chance I might assert my rights later on. They'll put it about that the wastrel brother passed away abroad." Her lips twisted. "So as a woman I can simply be dismissed, but as a man I have to die rather than threaten that idiot's career—? Such is the world, I suppose."

"And Mister Smith?"

"Will guarantee that I keep to the letter of our agreement, with the full weight of the Crown to be brought down upon me if Jonathan Chase shows up on their doorstep, drunk on gin and brandishing pistols or whatever they're imagining. Oh, Caro," she breathed, "it's all so, so *stupid*. What does it matter how I dress? Why can't I just be with you, and live my life?" Her eyes were welling. "It's as if, while I was away, Mama and Aggie got all these *ideas* in their heads ... when I first returned Aggie was furious at me, and my own mother said I was brainsick! When it was all her idea in the first place!"

She was weeping then. My darling Jo, who had stayed strong through so much—! I held her close, hushing her as she cried into my neck. "I can't bloody help it," she gasped against me, "I can't bloody help it if I love you, I can't bloody help it if the suits feel right ..."

"Of course not," I said firmly. "Of course you cannot help it, nor should you. This is *you*." I took her face in my hands. "This is who you are, this is how you were made. Who is anyone to question it?"

"So says the country girl," she said in a shuddering voice.

"So a wise woman taught me," I replied, kissing her. When we drew apart she wiped her nose on her sleeve and I groaned. "Though wise women also use handkerchiefs—! You don't have another shirt, remember?"

She stuck out her tongue at me, but then hugged me again. "I may have gotten a little tipsy," she mumbled into my hair. "I told Smith sending me after Edward Masterson was the best thing anyone's ever done for me."

I kissed her again and held her tight, though her words

provoked my unease. To vouch for a woman so defiant of convention was a risk, and Mr. Smith did not, to my knowledge, invite unnecessary risks. What would he ask of Jo in exchange for this?

But it was as Mr. Morrow said: our first task was to end any power Mr. Pestell might hold over Jo. We could reason out the situation with Mr. Smith later, when we were home at last.

Home. The thought made my heart constrict with longing. Soon, soon. If all went well with her family I would propose our departure, perhaps we could be away as soon as tomorrow …

Jo yawned against my neck. "He said I should try to sleep a little. He wants me sharp for this afternoon."

"Most sensible," I agreed, disentangling myself from her arms. "You take the bed. I will get some breakfast and take a walk."

"You will be there, won't you?" She clutched at my arm even as she lay down. "You must be there, Caroline. I won't sign anything without you."

At that I smiled warmly. "Thank you," I said, tucking the counterpane around her.

"I make stupid mistakes," she mumbled, her eyes drifting closed. "But I do try not to repeat them."

"Wise woman," I told her again.

In a moment her body had relaxed in much-needed slumber. I dressed swiftly and gathered up my cloak and bonnet. After a moment's thought I added Mr. Windham's knife to my pocket, as I was unfamiliar with the surrounding neighborhoods. With a last look at Jo's sleeping form, I slipped silently from the room.

I tiptoed past the dining room, where I could hear men's voices and the sound of dishes. I did not want yet to speak to anyone; I wanted time to think. Jo would be tired this afternoon, and struggling to think with her head rather than her heart. One of us had to have their wits about them, lest we lose any advantage.

Outside, the air was crisp but warming, and the sky showed blue through the scuttling clouds. I began walking down the street, following the rough map I now had in my head. Too, I realized, we were not so far from Tyburn and the Loveless house beyond. There might be some detail we overlooked in yesterday's confusion—and it would not hurt to have additional information for Mr. Smith, to ensure he remained an enthusiastic advocate.

So lost was I in my reasoning that I did not notice the woman until we barreled into each other. I started to apologize but found myself gazing at a familiar face. "Miss Morrow!" I exclaimed, while she cried, "Miss Daniels!" and quickly drew me into a doorway.

"Is Frannie with you?" she asked. Her lovely face was creased with worry. "He went out after supper last night, he said he would return but he never did."

"I haven't seen him, but he may be at Mister Smith's—I left without taking my leave, and there were a few gentlemen having breakfast."

"Ugh! That man." She stomped her foot, her eyes flashing with emotion. "He put our mother through it last night, he knows full well how frightened she is. There are so many stories, you see," she continued, "stories of being mistaken for a slave and being transported, no matter that we were born as free as anyone." She shook her head. "I know he has obligations to this man Smith, but what is Francis truly worth to him?"

I was so astonished at this speech that I could barely find the words to reply. "I—I had no idea," I said. "Surely you could demand your rights, show your papers?"

"What good are papers when you're halfway to the West Indies?" Her voice was starting to shake. "I just—I just want my family together, Miss Daniels. Surely you can understand. Is it so terrible to stay home, and take care of each other? What if I marry only to lose my brother?"

Still I could not think. That such a thing could happen, right here in London, under the very nose of the king? The machinations of Mr. Pestell seemed but a squabble in comparison. "Have you spoken to him about this?"

"Of course I have," she sniffed. "And he has told me not to be a ninny, and not to worry Mother, and he can handle himself, and a dozen other replies. But they took Benjamin, who played the fiddle down at the Red Lion. He was seen on a boat in the Thames calling for help, but it was gone by the time his friends got there."

She wiped roughly at her eyes, and I found my own welling in sympathy. To go through each day under the cloud of such fear? I could not fathom it, yet I knew better than to doubt her words. "Go to Mister Smith's," I said gently, handing her my handkerchief. "If Mister Morrow is not there they will know where he is, I'm certain of it."

"Thank you," she said in a trembling voice, dabbing at her eyes. "I'm sorry to be so overwrought, especially when you have your own worries—Frannie told me a little of Miss Chase's circumstances."

The warmth of feeling in her voice made my own tears start. She saw this and passed my handkerchief back to me, and we shared a shaky laugh. "I think your worries are of a far greater magnitude," I said. "But I appreciate your concern nonetheless. May we both know happier times, Miss Morrow."

She impulsively took my hand between hers and squeezed it. "I wish you all the best with Miss Chase."

"And I wish the same for you and your Gerald," I replied warmly.

With that we bid each other a shuddering farewell, then laughed again at our lingering emotions. Though I was once again left to my own thoughts, I could not help but glance back at her slim, erect form moving purposefully towards St. James' Square, how some of those passing her gave her startled looks, or sneered; how men did not step out of her path as they would for fair-skinned women, forcing her to weave and dodge as she made her way. *A slave, or as like*, the dastardly Mr. Hunt had assumed of Mr. Morrow. My own difficulties were numerous, but they paled in comparison to life in a world where your very body was a commodity.

As I resumed my journey, I realized then that here was a threat I could honestly fight, without compromise to my morals or my sense of self. Here was a real monster, not some brutish creature or corrupt men playing at power; a different kind of evil, insidious and devastating, one that required not mere thwarting but true change, with tangible benefit to hundreds, perhaps thousands. It seemed a better path than what we trod now, and I resolved to speak of it with Jo, when we next had time to ourselves.

It took longer than I anticipated to reach the Loveless house. I paused on the way, thinking to turn back and leave matters for another time, but I had already come so far. Would it not be quicker to go and then find a hackney coach for my return?

And then I realized I was mimicking Jo's own reasoning with her hasty flight to London, and I felt something ease a little inside me.

The house was as I remembered it, only brighter for the sunlight, yet the morning birdsong which had filled my walk ceased as soon as I reached the stone wall. Their silence gave me pause. In the past, such absence had been a warning of the Leviathan …

But there was no water for miles large enough for the beast, and I shook my head at my own foolishness. It was probably nothing more than a nearby cat, or a hungry raptor.

The grass was broken and trampled where we had circled the dwelling. I made my way slowly towards the door, holding up my skirts to keep them from becoming further stained—but then I stopped at the threshold.

The moss was streaked and crushed with the clear imprints of large boots. Too, the metal plate surrounding the keyhole was wiped clean, and the cobwebs above the door now hung in tatters.

Could it be Mr. Morrow? All of Miss Morrow's fears came back to me in a rush—oh, that I could reunite them, and ease her mind! Perhaps he had thought of something else, or thought to take a second look as I had. All was quiet, though—I heard no sounds from within. Yet the boot prints led up to the door, but not out again.

I looked around, but the nearest house was some ways away, shrouded by trees and with its shutters latched. Taking a deep breath, I placed my hand on the knob and let myself inside.

The first thing I noticed was the silence. Outside, it was the peace of an early morning; here in the house it hung thick and heavy, as thick as the dust that lay on the little table in the hall. Yet the dust on the staircase had been disturbed, with patches of wood showing through clearly on the banister and the risers. A recent investigation indeed.

"Mister Morrow?" I called softly. "Mister Morrow, it's Miss Daniels."

There was no response. I began climbing the stairs, pulling off my bonnet as I did so. I clutched it in one hand and with my other I gripped the knife tightly, keeping my steps as noiseless as possible. Every faint creak of the stairs seemed unnaturally loud. As the landing came into view I stopped abruptly, my breath catching as I took in the painting gazing back at me.

This was no pastoral, nor the churning coastline of my home. It was a full portrait of a woman, so lifelike she seemed about to lurch out of the canvas, her face lined and haughty, one hand curled into a fist. In her white dress, her pale skin and grey hair seemed almost ghostly; the only vivid colors were her reddened lips and the red rose pinned to her bodice. I knew at once that this was the mother we had glimpsed in the painting in Medby, now rendered as large as life, her watery blue eyes so vivid I expected them to blink.

And what of Penelope, conspiring with such a person? Oh, murderer she might be, yet I could not but feel an instinctive sympathy for the frail girl in Lady Audley's boudoir—and that terrified face I had glimpsed in the painting.

Slowly, I reached the landing and peeked in the nearest door. A bedroom, but as sparse as a cell and untouched for some time. The only hint of an occupant was a drab linen dress hanging from a peg and a small porcelain doll on the nightstand. The bed itself was as narrow as a coffin, wedged under the drafty window—was this how Penelope had lived?

It was then that I heard it: a rustle, so faint it might have been mere fancy—but I laid my bonnet on the bed and my cloak as well. Mr. Windham had taught me how easily such could be used against me in a fight. Renewing my grip on my knife, I went back to the landing. There was one other door on the far side of the stairs, past the painting.

As I brushed past the canvas, I felt a warmth on my arm, and tentatively laid my hand on the surface. Warmth, as I had felt at the Burton house, as if it had been in the sun for some time, though little light penetrated the gloomy hall. Warmth, and a damp softness, as if it were not paint at all but something else entirely—

I looked up at the face of Mrs. Masterson and for a moment it seemed her blue eyes were gazing down at me. I shifted my stance and it was but a trick of the light. Still, it made my skin rise to gooseflesh, and I quickly went to the second door and pushed it wide before entering.

"Mister Morrow?" I said. "Mister Morrow, are you here?"

Again I was answered with that heavy silence punctuated by a few buzzing flies, and a strange, unpleasant odor, as of rotting food. This room was much larger, running the length of the house, and it was no bedroom at all. Canvases leaned against the walls in stacks three and four deep, all manner of subjects, mostly unfinished. Sketches were tacked above the cold hearth, studies of faces, animals—

—and one large paper devoted to tentacles, their tapering shape and the little discs of flesh on their underside.

I looked around but there was no sign of Mr. Morrow, though the room felt more lived in than the rest of the house. There was a large table with pigments and oils, brushes in jars and a good many teacups; a shawl was bundled in the corner of an old sofa, its cushions creased with repeated use. But if Penelope was living and working here, how was she getting in?

Fascinated, I drew closer to the table. Here was the source of the strange odor, emanating from the tools of her craft. Not the pencils and charcoals, but not the teacups either; it came from the dried palette, where the paints had developed a lumpish texture as they dried. Flies flitted from one color to another like perverse bees. I picked up a rag but nearly gagged at the fresh odor and threw it in a corner. The jars contained strange brown flakes of varying sizes: one smelled of dried roses, another of leaves. There was a third, solid jar, of heavy ceramic, and it was with a sense of inevitable horror that I raised the lid …

And then I was heaving, my empty stomach wrenching itself. Rotten flesh and maggots, hundreds of them, sliding among what had become a jellied putrescence. I thought *not human*, and then shuddered that I knew enough to make the distinction. But whatever the source of the foul slime, I would wager much that it had come not from land but the sea.

My roiling stomach would not quiet. I shoved the lid back on and turned, thinking to get air, get back to the public house, think—

And then I saw the large painting hanging next to the open door.

It showed the hillside of all the others, only rendered as part of a larger landscape, showing the slope all the way down to the narrow beach. The sea with its white-capped surf lapped at strange, ovoid shapes clustered right at the edge of the sand. The spreading oak tree hung over the scene, though no family stood beneath it. On the far side of the tree the hillside sloped more gently, and a solitary figure seemed to be crawling towards the tree.

"Mister Morrow?" I exclaimed, my voice echoing in the stillness.

For it was Mr. Morrow, stripped to his shirt and with a distinct red spot on the white linen. He was stumbling, crawling, *moving* in the painting, the brushstrokes of his form rippling and sliding on the canvas as he staggered up the hill. "Mister Morrow," I cried again, but he did not seem to hear me, only kept heading unerringly towards the tree. The canvas was exuding heat, as if it were burning; I laid my hand atop his shimmering form and felt that strange, yielding dampness. I pushed, and my fingers slid into what felt for all the world like a layer of ground *meat*—

"Frannie!" I yelled, and the dark face turned towards me in surprise.

There was a rush of footsteps behind me. I turned to see a tangle of blond curls and a dirty sleeve before two hands struck my back and sent me flying into the painting.

CHAPTER XIV

Penelope

I flew through warm, moist air to land face-first on grass and, beneath it, hard earth. Then I was rolling, tumbling, my skirts tangling around my legs and my free hand unable to find purchase as I kept falling down, down. At last I struck bruising sand and skidded to a halt—and remained there, winded, my head spinning. My fist was thankfully rigid around the knife's hilt, and I focused on this sensation as one would an anchor. I became aware of water lapping, and the cries of birds, and a male voice bellowing *Daniels, Daniels,* but hollow and echoing, as if I was within a vast shell. Still, the sounds made me sit up and take stock of my surroundings.

Everything *felt* moist and soft, as if the world had been remade in damp wool: the air, the sand beneath me, the sparse grass that marked the start of the hill I had just tumbled down. My hair had come unpinned and was stuck to my face; it felt mushy as I combed it aside with my fingers, trying to see clearly—

—only to find myself gaping at the scene before me, for not twenty yards from the shoreline was the Leviathan.

It was half-submerged in the water, its tentacles pooling

on the surface of the churning sea, its vast yellow eye fixed upon the beachfront. The height of its head blotted out the lowering sky. Here were the dark, glistening scales I remembered from the bay; here was that intelligent gaze that had fixed upon me when I was thrown from its namesake vessel. Sea birds flew around it as they might circle a mountain, screeching as they clawed and pecked each other. To see the monster simply bobbing with the waves, the water slapping its sides as loud as gunshots and the birds like so many maddened flies, seemed an impossible thing, impossible to understand, impossible to witness. My body was nerveless; my sense of reason, of self, felt on the verge of collapse.

A wave receded and I saw then that its tentacles were not merely floating but undulating, caressing a dozen large, milky shapes half-buried in the sand at the water's edge. For a moment all I could think of was the balloons the butcher made from bladders, for the village children to play with …

But I knew, in truth, what I saw was nothing other than a clutch of eggs.

The tentacles were turning them, massaging them, pressing the soft white surfaces obscenely. The wet, sucking friction made me taste bile. An old, familiar panic was making my heart pound. They had driven the Leviathan off after the Thames blockade had failed—and somehow the monster had come *here*, to these fantastical waters.

To Arcadia.

I staggered to my feet, and only then did I see a figure moving among the eggs, seemingly unbothered by the meaty tentacles sliding around her. I held my knife ready and took a tentative step forward. I did not know what I would do, only that I had to do *something*. I walked forward on the wet sand, but it seemed as if I was wading through mud, so thick and wet was the air; each step only brought me a hand's breadth closer. Still I plodded forward. Now I could hear the tentacles splashing and rippling; now, too, I heard the woman singing:

Blow up the fire, my maidens,
Bring water from the well;
For a' my house shall feast this night,
Since my two sons are well.

"What are you doing?" I cried. "You must come away from there!"

The woman looked up at my cry and a smile peeled her lips from her teeth. She seemed a wild creature, her gray hair flying loose around her aged face, her thin, wet dress plastered to her body and knotted above her knees, yet I recognized her at once from the portrait in the hall. Mrs. Masterson. She stopped singing and slowly raised her arms towards me, as if in horrifying welcome. Then my reason did leave me for a moment, for in perfect mimicry two dark tentacles reached into the air. The birds began screaming, a relentless chorus.

"Will she make a covenant with thee?" she called, the words echoing, echoing. "Wilt thou take her for a servant forever?" Her voice rose in a kind of triumph. "Where will you be, when I remake the foundations of the world?"

As if in response, the creature bellowed, sending up a

cloud of spray and sand and making my head ring with the noise. I pressed my hands to my ears and clenched my eyes shut against the scouring onslaught. When next I could see, Mrs. Masterson had turned towards the Leviathan, those two raised tentacles now coiling around her as if embracing her, and I could not think, I could not think—

A hand seized my arm, spinning me about, and I ducked instinctively as Penelope swung a small sword right where my throat had been.

I threw myself forward, turning so my shoulder struck her in her chest. She grunted as we tumbled back onto the sand. I managed to seize her sword arm, but in turn she grabbed my wrist and twisted the knife down. We strained against each other, her body bucking again and again as she tried to throw me off. Tears spilling down her dirt-smeared face.

"Penelope!" I cried. "I'm here to—"

But at the sound of her name she screamed, and I flinched at the pain in her voice. She used my hesitation to roll us over. Now she was pinning me, her knee crushing my chest as we held each other's weapons at bay. Her lank, tangled hair hung before her face like tentacles of her own. I felt my grip weakening—

—and then a meaty fist shot across my field of vision, knocking Penelope off me. I scrambled into a crouch with my knife ready. Mr. Morrow, his face ashen and sweaty, slumped next to me. "Was calling you," he managed, gasping. "She's ... moving in and out ... somehow ..."

Alarmed, I looked where Penelope had landed: gone. Around us the shimmering world suddenly took on a new light. How many paintings were there, potential doors for her to leave and return through?

My wits, at least, were returning. I spared a glance for the beachfront, but while the eggs remained, both Mrs. Masterson and the creature had vanished. Had it not been for those soft, glistening forms I might have believed the whole episode a dream. I turned again to Mr. Morrow, forcing away the arm that he had wrapped protectively around his torso, only to wince at the dark stain spread over his shirt. "We must get you to a doctor," I said. When my words had no response I added, "if you die here your sister will be furious."

That provoked a weak smile, but a smile nonetheless. I tucked the knife in my pocket and drew his arm around my shoulders, and with a grunt I managed to get us both upright. We started staggering up the hill, step by precarious step, but too soon he fell. When I started to pull him to his feet again, he shook his head. "Get help," he whispered.

I looked around at the blurring hillside, the oak tree spreading overhead. From our elevation I saw the coast curving unbroken in both directions, a great arc of surf as far as I could see. "There is no help to get, Mister Morrow," I said grimly. "There is only ourselves."

He inhaled, as if about to argue, but instead staggered into a crouch. I did the same, and we managed to propel ourselves further up the hillside, though each step made him whine in pain. "If we can only figure out where the openings are," I said, trying to distract us both. "Do the paintings stay open, or do they only open for Penelope?"

"They do as they're told," a woman said. "Creations always mimic their makers."

We both froze and looked up, Mr. Morrow teetering. Penelope stood at the crest of the hill, the short sword held out before her like a dagger. Now I could see her more clearly: she wore a filthy smock and trousers, and her blond hair was knotted and wild. In this strange place she looked at one moment clearly present, the next blurred and muddied. Yet she was not much older than her portrait, and that gave me a small hope.

"Penelope, we mean you no harm," I said, raising my voice to be sure it carried. Mr. Morrow coughed beside me but I ignored him. "We only want to ask you about the nine men, and what they did."

At her name she flinched, and then a hard, thin smile spread across her face. "You mistake me, madame," she said. "There is no one here by that name."

"Then who are you?" Again Mr. Morrow coughed and I hissed at him, why wouldn't the infuriating man stay silent? "For you are very like Penelope. I've seen her picture."

Her sneering expression never wavered, but the sword wobbled, just a little. "You're the one who killed her sons."

"Penelope—"

"Stop calling me that!" The sword cut a line in the air before resuming its upright stance. She started to say something else, then laughed instead. "My name is Missus Loveless," she declared. "Or *the girl,* if you like. *The girl* will marry him. *The girl* will be our vessel." She took a step towards us. "Like a nun, she said: a vessel for a higher purpose."

"But you are not a *vessel*, you are Penelope," I said quickly. Mr. Morrow's hand crept into my pocket and seized my knife. "You don't have to serve her anymore." When she took another step forward I readied myself. "Not her, and not the monster."

With a cry Penelope lunged forward. Mr. Morrow shoved us apart, so that we each lurched sideways; she skidded between us and he sliced at her back, sending her tumbling down the hill with a shriek of pain. I caught him by the arm and hauled him up, watching as Penelope hit the sand much as I had done. At once she was on her feet, screaming. It was a terrible sound, full of pain and fury—

And then she ran into a shimmering patch of air and vanished.

"The tree," I said, pulling at Mr. Morrow again. "We need the vantage." But he only slumped to the ground. When I bent over him his face was glistening with sweat, his eyelids fluttering. The stain on his shirt had become large, so very large.

Gritting my teeth, I caught him under the armpits and began dragging him up the hillside. Perhaps in the end it would make no odds, but every instinct I possessed told me the tree was our safest place. Sweat poured off me as I pulled Mr. Morrow's dead weight—who knew that men were so heavy?— while straining to hear Penelope should she attack again.

It sounded as if the air was calling *Caro, Caro*, and I shook my head at my own foolishness: this was no time for fancies.

Below me, Mr. Morrow moaned. I glanced over my shoulder at the looming trunk. "Nearly there," I gasped. "Nearly there." Though how that was supposed to reassure him, I could not say. In all likelihood I was merely altering the location of our demise.

My foot struck the first root. I eased Mr. Morrow against the trunk when something struck me in the head, sending me to my knees. I looked up just in time to see the sword come down and rolled aside, my skirt tangling around my legs. I reached for my knife but realized it had slipped from Mr. Morrow's grasp. Again Penelope attacked and I tried to kick myself away but my dress had become binding, I could only fling out an arm—

But instead of a blow, there was a volley of curses, and I looked up to see Penelope smacking and punching an arm around her throat, an arm that was connected to a shadowy figure. From behind it Jo darted towards me, a rope tied around her waist. "Caroline!" she cried, pulling me up and away. "Darling, are you all right—"

"I am fine," I gasped, placing a name to the shadow: George, from Callisto House. "But Mr. Morrow is bleeding—dying—"

George expertly twisted Penelope's arm behind her back and she wailed and dropped her sword. Jo gave her rope two sharp tugs: now I saw that it receded into the shifting gloom and then seemed to stop abruptly, as if someone had cut it. "Get her back to Smith," Jo said, "and tell them Morrow is badly hurt, and to fetch a doctor."

With a nod and a wink at me, George began marching Penelope down the hill, following the rope. Near its floating end I saw a hand appear and wave them close, like some fantastical conjuring trick, but Jo tugged on my arm to get my attention. She had taken off her coat and was holding it against Mr. Morrow's chest. I knelt beside her, pressing where she placed my hands. As she felt Mr. Morrow's pulse I whispered, "What of your family?"

At that she grinned at me, and my heart leapt. "Oh, they are all here, though Mama fainted when she saw the paintings start to move." The rope suddenly jerked twice. She looked over her shoulder. "Dangerous to move him in this state, but we cannot let ourselves become trapped. Have you ever moved an injured man?"

When I shook my head, she showed me how we would arrange our arms, then gave Mr. Morrow a hard shake. "Morrow, wake up! You're too damn heavy to sleep through this." When his eyelids fluttered she shook him again and they opened completely, even managing a faint, outraged squint. "Good man. We're going to lift you, but I need you to say if you're falling or sliding. All right?"

His head rolled and he squinted at me, as if to say *are you party to this?* But Jo was already sliding her arms under him. I did the same and we locked together, forming a kind of seat. On her count we staggered to our feet, and began stumbling down the hillside, steadying his weight between us. To distract myself from the pain in my arms I looked ahead at the rope, whose slack was disappearing into a muddy patch of air as swiftly as we were moving. It was a strange sight, both frightening and enthralling. The thought came, unbidden: *yet another thing to dream about*—and as if prompted, the upper part of Charlie's body appeared, his arms outstretched to us.

"Hurry," he cried, and Jo quickened her steps, forcing me

to hurry as well. Silently I prayed for solid footing, and was rewarded with such up to the moment when we were close enough for him to seize Mr. Morrow's shoulders. My ankle caught in a divot and twisted, so that I stumbled through that fleshy thickness and into the drier air of Mr. Smith's parlor. Jo tried to both steady Mr. Morrow and catch my arm, but in my fall I let go of Mr. Morrow completely, causing Charlie to topple beneath the sudden weight. The four of us tumbled to the floor in a pile of filthy, bloody limbs, the rope coiled about us. I caught my breath, then looked up into the shocked face of Mr. Pestell, and for the life of me I will never know what caused me to say what I did.

"Pardon me," I said. "We haven't met properly. I'm Jo's partner, Caroline."

CHAPTER XV

Closing Doors

$\mathcal{I}$n the afternoon sunlight, Penelope looked ill. There was a feverish cast to her waxen skin and deep circles under her eyes, and her colorless lips were cracked from dryness. She had combed her hair into some semblance of order and wrapped herself in a quilt despite the warmth of the room. Only her foot, chained to the bedpost, emerged from the mass of cloth. Her gaze flitted listlessly from one side of the room to the other, never settling. When I entered, she barely glanced at me, though Mr. Windham stood up with obvious relief.

"Perhaps she will listen to you," he said in a low voice. "Your story has alarmed Mister Smith, yet she will not speak of what you saw, nor give us any information about Missus Masterson. Without some excuse to keep her, he will be hard-pressed to turn her over to the magistrate, and it will be the gallows for her."

"Are there no mitigating circumstances?" I whispered.

"She made no attempts to disguise herself when she entered the houses, and that Gribble provided a precise description." He nodded at the door. "With the portrait from Callisto House? She'll have a difficult time protesting her innocence, even if she had the will to do so."

I scowled, but I knew he was right. The portrait was damning, yet it could not be unseen. Lady Audley and George had come ostensibly to submit it for evidence, but also to bring a collection they had taken up for Jo. Now they were lingering in the dining room. Jo's mother was still in a faint in the room I had slept in, and Miss Morrow with her brother in yet another bedroom, where a doctor had sewn his wounds and given him a sleeping draught.

Downstairs, Jo was in the study with her sister and Mr. Pestell. Twice, I had gone to enter, and twice I had hesitated. They were not yet meeting with Mr. Smith, what conversation might I be interrupting with my presence? Instead I had found myself wandering until I ended up here.

Mr. Windham gave my arm a squeeze and held out a chair for me. I settled in it, then simply watched as Penelope's eyes darted from place to place. The quilt over her body kept moving, as if she were clawing at herself.

"I've seen it before, you know," I said then, conversationally. "Leviathan. I have been close to it thrice now."

She tittered at my words, but said nothing.

"How did the Leviathan get to Arcadia, Penelope?"

At that she tittered again. "Is that where it is?" she asked, her eyes dancing from the floor to the wall to the window. "I thought it was taking the waters in Bath."

I smiled before I could stop myself. "Edward Masterson told me it is the source of English power—"

"Fools," she interrupted. "All those men, only seeing what is here." She held her hand in front of her face. "Always on about *England, England*. England isn't real, you know. England is just a *word.*"

"But Arcadia is real?"

"From the mountains to the sea, until the covenant was broken and the waters came." She recited the words in a singsong. "No England, no France. Just Arcadia."

"Did Missus Masterson tell you that story?" I asked.

"Stories tell us who we are," she replied.

"And who are you, Penelope?"

"Who am I?" She began tittering again. "I am nothing! I am the serpent's tooth. I'm the slattern who will draw your picture for a penny. I am Richard's wife. I am the *vessel.*" She raised her leg and shook her manacle at me. "How could I harm anyone? I don't even have a name."

"You don't need a name to kill someone," I pointed out. For a moment my mind flashed back to the *Leviathan,* the man shuddering beneath me—

But that didn't matter here, now.

"Of course," I mused, "the men had names, did they not? Lord Otterburn. Sir Lewis Burton. Gerald Vacher. Good men, each—"

I was interrupted by her bark of laughter. "Good men," she sneered. "There is *good,* and there are *good men,* and they are not the same." She raised her chin and studied the ceiling, then followed the picture rail. "No man dares to remake the covenant."

"But Missus Masterson dares," I said, feeling more certain now. "And you've been helping her—by painting Arcadia. By painting the Mastersons *into* Arcadia."

She looked at her lap, saying nothing, the blanket shifting

and twisting as if alive.

"And somehow the pictures become more than pictures," I pressed. "You had things in your house—petals, leaves, but also flesh. Was it the Leviathan's flesh? Did Missus Masterson teach you—"

Penelope lunged forward and clapped her hand over my mouth, her eyes focused on my face and wide with fright. "Shut up," she hissed. "For the love of God, shut up!" When I only stared at her, astonished, her eyes began to fill. *"She can hear us,"* she whispered.

At once my mind flew to the paintings, still in the parlor below us. I lowered my eyes to the floor, and when I looked up again Penelope nodded, once. There were footsteps in the hall, and in an eyeblink Penelope was once more swaddled in her blanket and looking vacantly about herself.

A swift knock was followed by the door opening. Oliver stood there, a tray with three sherry glasses balanced on one hand. "Your lady would like you to join her," he said formally, then winked at me. "I think terms have been agreed upon—?"

I shook myself. I felt as if I was awakening from a dream, a terrible dream. "Yes," I said, rising. "Yes, I'm coming."

"Fear not, I shall keep her company until Charlie returns," Oliver said. "He is gathering the remaining paintings, but should be back this evening." He handed me a glass. "I think everyone could use one of these—even our prisoner."

"Is he bringing the paintings here?"

"I believe they are bound for the carriage house." He glanced at Penelope, but she was staring at a bedpost.

"Good. The others should be put there as well," I said in

a low voice. "They may still—open."

"Just as Jeremy suspected," Oliver replied, his voice equally as low. "Great minds, Miss Daniels." He gestured to the hall. "Go on, then, and don't give any of this another thought. You and Miss Chase have more pressing matters to attend to."

On my way to the study I was accosted by George, who took me to one side, his expression strained. "Has it been decided, then? Has she signed anything?"

"I don't know," I said, a little irritated. "I am just going in now."

Still he would not let go of my arm; his dark eyes had a feverish urgency. "You won't leave her, will you?" he asked in a whisper. "They will take everything from her. It is vital that you do not leave her."

"Of course not," I exclaimed. "Why would you even think such a thing?"

But he released my arm. He rolled his shoulders, the same stiffness he had shown at Callisto House. "Good," he said. "Good."

"George, are you all right?" I asked.

"Old injury." He smiled tightly at my concern. "I tried to marry and ended up in the stocks instead, Miss Daniels. It's why we have to look out for each other, no matter what." He bowed, then, almost carelessly: "Lottie says we are to go, but if you need a place tonight, you can come to my flat. It's small but I can make room." Before I could reply he ducked down the hall, as if embarrassed by his own generosity. I had no more time to think on his words, for the study door was open and Mr. Smith was impatiently gesturing me inside.

They had roused Mrs. Chase for our meeting, which was held with all the formality of reading a will. I sat beside Jo, holding her hand tight, for its trembling was the only sign of any distress on her part. Her face was an expressionless mask. Her family sat across from us, in chairs just out of reach, creating a strangely empty space between us. Mr. Smith and the lawyer he had procured sat behind his desk, Mr. Smith watching us silently while the lawyer sorted through several papers and made notations on them.

"Your sister has asked me to make one more appeal, now that your *friend* is present," Mr. Pestell said. "These activities of yours, the company you keep, are all clearly unfit for any woman, much less the relation of one who will share my station in life. She fears that matters have come to a precipice, and after today you will be lost to her. So I will say, one last time, that we will welcome her sister Joanna Chase with open arms, and happily restore her to her proper role."

"My sister," Jo snapped, "has a voice, and can say these things for herself."

"Joanna!" her mother cried, but could not form any further admonition save to wring her hands.

"Jo, he is my fiancé," Agnes said. "He speaks for us both." She dabbed at her eyes. "I want my children to know their aunt," she continued, her voice throbbing. "I want you home and safe."

"And what I want," Jo replied, "is to make my own choices, and to be afforded respect even when they differ from yours." There was a quiet fury in her voice, and in return tears began running freely down her sister's face. I understood then that their earlier conversation had been a painful one.

"Even when your choices threaten our standing, and thus our livelihood?" Mr. Pestell's voice was cool.

"Of course not—" Mrs. Chase began, but Jo cut in, "They are as much a threat as you permit them to be, Pestell."

"May I remind you all that I have pressing matters to attend to?" Mr. Smith said then. "Can we proceed?"

Jo gave her sister a last, hard look. "Let's," she said. Her hand shuddered in mine, however, and I surreptitiously rubbed my thumb over hers, trying to put in that one small gesture all the comfort I knew she needed.

And it was something I would never forget, I knew, not for whatever allotment of years I had before me: how it felt to watch Mr. Pestell, Mr. Smith, and the lawyer carefully chip away at the family ties that bound Jo to her mother and sister. At each item in the contract the lawyer would pause, while Jo and Mr. Pestell debated the matter in soft, cool voices. The principles, I swiftly realized, were never in doubt. Jo was quibbling out of pride, little more, and perhaps also to further needle her mother, who kept uttering exclamations such as, "Joanna would never!" and, "no daughter of mine would think of it!" For as Jo pointed out, over and over, there had been no quarrel with her behavior when it served the purpose of preserving their income. Was she supposed to simply change at their every whim?

And when it was all over, the woman I loved had kept her birth name—and nothing else. No claim to what little property her father had left them, or the firm she had guided back into solvency; no right to act upon the many transactions and deeds she had signed as Jonathan; no contact with either her mother or sister save in response to their invitation, and following their explicit terms. All of which was guaranteed by Mr. Smith, who took responsibility for her behavior and any appearance of the name Chase in less than salubrious circumstances.

Jo was free—free of both the restrictions Mr. Pestell would have inflicted on her, and of the family she had worked so hard to care for. Never had I seen her look so defeated. At some point, too, her sister had begun openly weeping, and it was with red, swollen eyes that she darted from the room the moment Jo signed the contract. Her mother left and did not look back. Mr. Pestell gave us a curt nod, then leaned across the desk and shook Mr. Smith's hand once.

And then they were gone, perhaps forever. Jo stayed where she was seated, staring at the empty chairs as if she wanted to argue further. Mr. Smith whispered to the lawyer and they left the room with swift bows. It was with some difficulty that I turned Jo to me, laying my hand on her cheek. Her eyes filled and then my darling burst into tears, and all I could do was hold her.

It was late that night when I left our room to search for supper. Jo had been too distraught to eat, and I too worried to leave her. She seemed to want neither conversation nor reassurance, yet kept rousing herself from her own thoughts to see that I was nearby. It was not until she had finally fallen asleep that I felt comfortable leaving her side—only to nearly trip over a basket placed right outside our door, containing some bread and sliced meat, a little pot of salad, and a corked bottle of wine. Oliver's doing, I suspected, and I silently thanked him as I took up the basket, pausing at a faint sound coming from the far end of the hall.

Singing. A woman, singing.

Placing the basket in our room, I tiptoed towards the sound. Past the bedroom where Mr. Morrow slept, his sister tucked in the chair beside his bed, covered with a shawl; past a closed door that I suspected was Mr. Smith's room, though it had not once been open since I arrived. Had it only been two days ago? It felt a lifetime—as I suspected all his investigations did.

At the far end of the hall was the room where Penelope was being kept, the door partway open. I glimpsed a fire banked low, Mr. Windham sprawled asleep on a couch, and Penelope still sitting upright in her quilted swaddling, rocking back and forth and singing under her breath:

I wish the wind may never cease,
Nor fashes in the flood,
Till my two sons come hame to me,
In earthly flesh and blood.

She broke off and looked at the door, though I stood in darkness. "She knows who you are now," she said. "She'll be waiting for you."

Frightened, I hurried back to our own bedroom, trying to move as swiftly as possible without making noise. I thought again of the grey-haired woman on the beach, and those vast, unnatural eggs. Only then did I realize that the song was the same one Mrs. Masterson had been singing.

I ate a little and coaxed Jo into taking a few bites of bread and a sip of wine, then we coiled in each other's arms, exhausted by the day. I thought her asleep when she whispered in my neck, "Caroline?"

"What is it, darling?" I, too, whispered, though no one could hear us.

"Is it all right, if I—if I come home with you? Only I still have to be paid for this, and George's wallet will just cover the journey north—"

I hushed her then, kissing her, holding her close. "Never ask that again," I whispered fiercely. "Never ask that. It's not home without you there."

The answer seemed to reassure her, and she soon fell asleep once more, but I fought my own drowsiness, dreading what I might dream. I feared revisiting Penelope's furious attack, or the Leviathan reaching for me with those sickening tentacles. I feared, too, what might have happened if I had made it within arm's length of Mrs. Masterson. *She'll be waiting for you,* and with what dark intent? The Masterson brothers' actions had seemed disjointed, two separate, yet monstrous agendas. Now I wondered if their mother was the hidden unity behind them. Arcadia, too; I had to speak with Mr. Smith about Arcadia, he needed to question Penelope further …

But when I finally slept that night, I dreamed not of monsters or Mastersons but my own mother, gone nearly two decades now. How she had looked that day at Harkworth Hall, how safe and healing her embrace had been when I was finally rescued from the folly. Her arms around me made me weep in my dreams, for I was grown and found, found once more. Then it was not my mother holding me but Jo, and I looked over her shoulder to see both my parents walking towards the cliff edge, as if to throw themselves into the churning waters of the bay.

I awoke then to the grey light of dawn, my face soaked with tears and a cold certainty breaking my heart. Before Jo awakened I had already packed my things. She took one look at my face and asked me what had happened.

"I don't know," I said, "but I have a terrible feeling—" and then I could say no more. Bless her, she did not press me, only kissed me and then set to dressing. Thus neither of us were surprised when Charlie knocked at our door, and handed me the letter that had been sent with all possible haste:

Come as soon as you can. He has taken a turn. We fear the worst.

I missed my father's passing by four hours.

CHAPTER XVI

Farewells

*G*rief cast the world in shadow. Grief hollowed me and
filled me with its cold dullness, weighting my limbs
and mind, leaving me stupefied. I lost all track of time; there
was only the dullness, punctuated by bouts of weeping that
wracked my frame and left me exhausted. I had imagined
many times my father's passing, to prepare myself for the
blow of it, but my imagination had failed me utterly. My
first view of his body convulsed me as no sickness had ever
done. He was so small and forlorn, and when they told me he
had passed alone—! I felt as if I, too, were dying in that moment, and all my reason left me. When I knew myself again
the world was grey and lifeless, and I grey and lifeless in it.

There were people, and then there were no people, and
then there were people again. The coffin came and I convulsed once more, I could not bear to watch him placed in
it. It was then, I think, that Jo took charge. I remember her
voice often, quietly giving instructions, presenting me with
brief statements: *Caro, we will bury him on the morrow; Caro,
it is time to dress; Caro, the vicar is here.* Much of those days
became a blur, and perhaps that was for the best.

What I do remember clearly, every detail etched forever

in my mind: how we buried him on a warm afternoon that started to drizzle as the vicar spoke, and then as they lowered the coffin, Jo began to read. It had been one of my father's few instructions for his funeral, and I was deeply grateful that she had remembered. *I've already made my peace with God*, he would say. *Spare me the Bible, and read me some bloody poetry instead.*

> *Like as the waves make towards the pebbl'd shore,*
> *So do our minutes hasten to their end;*
> *Each changing place with that which goes before,*
> *In sequent toil all forwards do contend.*
> *Nativity, once in the main of light,*
> *Crawls to maturity, wherewith being crown'd,*
> *Crooked eclipses 'gainst his glory fight,*
> *And Time that gave doth now his gift confound.*
> *Time doth transfix the flourish set on youth*
> *And delves the parallels in beauty's brow,*
> *Feeds on the rarities of nature's truth,*
> *And nothing stands but for his scythe to mow:*
> *And yet to times in hope my verse shall stand,*
> *Praising thy worth, despite his cruel hand.*

And then, the rain pelting harder, we threw the first spadefuls of dirt on his coffin. Jo turned me away and we went home.

We went home, but it was no longer home. My father was gone and the heart of the house with him. Too, the letter to my cousin had been sent. It would be some months before he arrived, but the days now stretched before me with dull finality. Jo threw herself into assessing the property and his papers, often shutting herself in his study for hours. I set myself to sorting my father's clothes, but though I know he would have wanted them to be passed on I could not bear to part with them. They bore all the marks of his wear, the creases and worn edges, the bits of paper and pencil in his pockets. God help me, they *smelled* of him …

I was weeping, weeping over his old brown suit when there was a knock at the bedroom door. I looked up to see Dr. Denham, his hat in his hand.

"Pardon me," he said. "Only I am returning to Medby on the morrow, and Mrs. Simmons mentioned you were sleeping poorly?"

I stared at him, tears running down my face, utterly astonished at his presence—I knew my father had corresponded with him after we left Medby, but to see him here? Now?—and then I remembered: he had been here that first, hazy night, for the Simmonses had sent for him as well as myself.

Swiftly, he shut the door and steered me into a chair—the same chair I had sat on at my father's bedside. I could not help myself. I clutched the suit to my chest and wept hard, as hard as I had the first few days.

"Should I fetch Miss Chase—" but he broke off as I shook my head, though I could not explain my instinctive refusal. Instead he laid a hand on my shoulder, warm and comforting, and waited through my tears. As I finally began to quiet, a handkerchief appeared before me and I pressed it to my eyes.

Gingerly he sat down on the bed, looking to me as if for approval. Only when I gave him a small nod did he settle there completely. "Miss Daniels," he began, "your grief does you credit, but I know in my heart your father would not want you to suffer so."

"I wasn't here," I blurted out. My voice was loud and shuddering in the room, startling us both. I had not expected to speak, but the words seemed to come from someplace deep inside me. "I wasn't here and he died alone, with no one beside him, no one to hold his hand, to tell him it would be all right …"

I began sobbing again. The suit was taken from my arms and then Dr. Denham hugged me, rubbing my back as I wept into his shoulder like a child. A small part of my mind cried out for Jo, but again I shied away from asking for her.

When at last I quieted once more, my face swollen and my breath ragged, he laid his hands briefly on my face, as if I were indeed a child. "My dear Miss Daniels," he said, his own eyes overbright. "Even if you had been home, you most likely would not have been at his side. We three were here that morning; we took turns sitting with him. He seemed well on the way to recovery, so much so that we debated sending you a second message, to tell you the worst had passed. It was Mr. Simmons' turn when it happened. Your father sent him downstairs to fetch a glass of sherry, and Mr. Simmons did so, without pause or distraction. When he returned, your father was gone. It was the work of a minute. I doubt Theophilus knew what was happening. Even if you had been in this very chair, there would have been no time for parting words."

I could only stare at him, piecing together the scene he presented. I could hear my father's voice asking for a sherry as a treat, to celebrate beating the Reaper once more, a sherry and an article read to him while he napped …

"They—the Simmonses—they did not say," I finally whispered.

"Actually, Miss Daniels, they did, only I think you were too grief-stricken to hear it." He wiped a tear away and I held out his sodden handkerchief without thinking. We both laughed a little. "He was so proud of you," he continued. "His only regret, I think, was that he had not given full consideration to your feelings in the past, and spent so much time trying to foist his own ideas of a happy life upon you, when he knew in his heart you would never want to marry a man."

Again I stared at him, now completely astonished. That my father knew! That he had confided so in Dr. Denham! That he had looked at me so many times knowing, that he had truly seen me—oh, it set me to tears again, but they felt different this time, as if cleansing some old, festering wound.

Dr. Denham patted my hands. "Keep the handkerchief," he said with a little smile as he rose. "I was going to leave you a cordial," he added, "but perhaps this will be enough to help you rest?"

"Thank you," I said earnestly. "Thank you, I—" Impulsively, I rose and flung my arms around him. "Thank you," I whispered once more.

He hugged me again, then took up his hat. "I'll show myself out," he said. At the door, however, he paused. "I understand you have to leave here," he said. "It may have too many associations, but know that Medby would welcome the return of the charming Mister Read and his pretty wife."

Jo. I nodded at his words, but my mind had flown to her. The greyness was lifting, and taking with it some of my guilt—for it was guilt as well as grief that had weighted me so, guilt at not being by his side, at not being the daughter I thought he wanted. I found myself longing to tell Jo, to hold her and be held in turn.

I went through the house but did not find her, nor was she in the gardens. The horse and carriage were gone; perhaps she had left on an errand. She had spoken of posting papers to London.

For the first time I realized how fresh and warm the air was. It heated me through, setting my skin alight and drying the tears in my throat. I felt like I, too, had been ill, and was only now recovering.

I started walking, as I had not done since before London, striking out on the footpaths I knew so well. I found myself remembering childhood walks with my father, the two of us rambling while he told me his favorite stories from history, or explained the workings of Parliament, or tested me on the names of the plants we passed. I thought, too, of my early womanhood, and how I had lost some of that rapport in exchange for taking on more household duties—and I wondered now if I had done so to avoid discussing marriage, or from some lingering pain over my mother's passing, or a mixture of both.

These thoughts so engrossed me that I did not realize I

had headed for the bay until I was nearly upon it. I had avoided the coast after our encounters with the Masterson brothers. Now I found myself drinking up its beauty like a traveler returning after a long absence. How had I let those evil men take this from me? This, I thought, was another way to fight, one that did not require knives or monsters: holding onto the beauty that was rightfully shared by all.

I heard my name and turned to see Jo, hurrying towards me, her lovely face creased with worry, her hair loose and blowing about her and torched by sunlight. I ran to her and embraced her as I had never dared before, and as we tumbled into the windswept grass I let my wounds begin to heal at last.

It was the sun's heat that stirred me awake from where I drowsed in her arms, both of us half-naked and utterly content. She had made us a pillow from her coat, and as I turned to kiss her bare shoulder I heard paper crinkle in her pocket. I drew out an envelope and at once knew the handwriting.

"Fear not," Jo murmured, "I have already drafted my refusal."

"But—"

"You are more important." She sat up, her skin rising to gooseflesh as a breeze blew over us. "You are the most important thing," she said, and there was a tremor in her voice now. "Had I realized this earlier you—your *father*—"

She wiped roughly at her face, but when I laid a hand on her arm she shook it off. "I will never forgive myself," she gasped. "I will never forgive myself for taking you away when he needed you. Smith can go hang for all I care. I—"

I sat up next to her and, keeping my gaze on the grass, I repeated what Dr. Denham had told me. Jo began crying halfway through, her own tears started mine, and it was so, so *good* to weep together, to wrap our arms around each other and just cry. This was not the terrible dark grief of before, it was something cleaner, brighter.

"Smith can still go hang," she finally said as she felt her coat pockets and came up with a handkerchief. She handed it to me, and when I had finished wiping my eyes she blew her nose violently.

I took up the letter and read it through. "He wants to release Penelope?" I exclaimed. "He would use the girl as, as *bait*? There must be some other way …"

But even as I spoke, I was back in that little room with Penelope. *No England, no France. Just Arcadia.* Somehow the Leviathan had crossed from the Channel to the waters in the painting, and there was no canvas in the world large enough for such a creature. Arcadia had to be real. There was no other explanation.

Where will you be, when I remake the foundations of the world?

"I neither know nor care," Jo snapped. "Morrow can do whatever needs doing, or Windham. He doesn't need us."

"Jo." I ignored her groan and continued, "Mister Smith served as your guarantee. If you don't go, what might he do? Think on it," I pressed as she opened her mouth. "Think on it, because that settlement was hard won, Joanna Chase. Would you risk that now?"

"I won't leave you," she said stubbornly. "And I won't drag you into yet another mess just because this damn family doesn't know when it's beaten."

"Language," I said, looking at the bay. Not quite home anymore, but perhaps that might change, if I returned here someday.

It struck me then: I could just go. I could follow Penelope, or go abroad, or anyplace for that matter. I could go without worry for my father, for our accounts, for the house … I was heartbroken and empty and yet somehow also free, as I had never been before.

"Jo," I began slowly, thinking as I spoke. "Those shapes I spoke of? I am certain they were eggs. So many eggs, and they were so, so *large* …" I looked at her. "They cannot be loosed upon the world. The Leviathan cannot be loosed upon the world, not again. We have to stop it, once and for all."

Her lips parted, but she said nothing. She took my hand in hers.

"Besides," I added, "you do realize, if Mister Morrow ends up saving England, he will become absolutely insufferable. We owe it to his sister to save him from himself."

She stared at me for a heartbeat longer and then started laughing, and I laughed too, laughing and weeping as I pressed myself against her once more. She lowered me down into the thick, waving grass and her face was ringed by clouds and blue, blue sky, and as her mouth settled upon mine I thought *this is life, this is life*, and I gave myself over to it.

Misses Chase and Daniels will return in

A Shining Path

ACKNOWLEDGEMENTS

This one was a beast. Personal matters kept me from tackling the final chapters for months, and when it was all finally written I found myself in circumstances that lost me weeks of pay while I navigated the murky waters of worker's compensation. To come so far, and yet be stymied so close to the final draft, drove me to do something unprecedented: I reached out to my newsletter for help, and help they did. I am deeply, deeply grateful to Marie Blanchet, Jean Blythe, Stephanie A. Cain, Sian M. Jones, E.M. Markoff and Gabriel Markoff, Ellen Morais, Russell and Karen Nohelty, Loren Rhoads, and Dennis C. Smith, Sr., as well as those who asked to remain anonymous. That this book exists at all is due in no small part to their generous donations.

As always, this book was bettered by the editorial efforts of Kat Howard and Charlotte Ashley. Manu Velasco gave me a careful sensitivity reading that improved the book immeasurably. Najla Qamber crafted the cover and interpreted my vague directions with patience and aplomb. Nada Qamber withstood all my last-minute layout fiddling with her usual fortitude. I am lucky to be the beneficiary yet again of such a skilled, generous team.

And then, of course, there's you, dear reader. If you are reading these words it's likely this is your third adventure with Caro and Jo. I hope you'll stick around for the last.

ABOUT THE AUTHOR

L.S. Johnson was born and raised in New York and now lives in California. Besides the Chase & Daniels novellas, she has published over thirty short stories in such venues as *Beneath Ceaseless Skies*, *The Threepenny Review*, and *Year's Best Weird Fiction*. Her first collection, *Vacui Magia: Stories*, won the North Street Book Prize and was a finalist for the World Fantasy Award. Her second collection, *Rare Birds: Stories*, is now available. You can sign up for her mostly-monthly newsletter at www.traversingz.com.

WITHDRAWN

Made in the USA
Monee, IL
22 July 2020

36849111R00104